"I know ... **relations**...

"Business only," Curt repeated. A moment later he gave a reluctant nod. "All right."

"Great," Cammie said. "Let's shake on it." She held out her hand.

He shook his head. "No touching. Not even a handshake. I'll let myself out. Good night, Cammie."

He left without a backward glance.

Two more weeks until the wedding and she wouldn't have to see him except now and then, when they ran into each other.

Meanwhile, she would make herself stop wanting him. *She would!*

Somehow.

Dear Reader,

This is the second of the three stories set in the fictitious town of Cranberry, Oregon (the first was *The Man She'll Marry*, which is still available from some of the e-booksellers). Times have changed since that first book. With the employee-owned factory thriving, Cranberry is growing and is as popular with tourists as ever.

Fran Bishop and the Oceanside Bed and Breakfast are back, this time for a wedding in the great room. I had a lot of fun with this story featuring Cammie, an events planner, and Curt, a photographer, who once were friends but have had a falling-out.

I hope you enjoy their story. I would love to hear from you. Visit my Web site at www.annroth.net and/or e-mail me at ann@annroth.net.

Happy reading!

Ann Roth

It Happened One Wedding

ANN ROTH

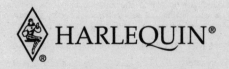

HARLEQUIN®

TORONTO • NEW YORK • LONDON
AMSTERDAM • PARIS • SYDNEY • HAMBURG
STOCKHOLM • ATHENS • TOKYO • MILAN • MADRID
PRAGUE • WARSAW • BUDAPEST • AUCKLAND

ISBN-13: 978-0-373-75163-1
ISBN-10:   0-373-75163-X

IT HAPPENED ONE WEDDING

This edition published by arrangement with Harlequin Books S.A.

® and TM are trademarks of the publisher. Trademarks indicated with ® are registered in the United States Patent and Trademark Office, the Canadian Trade Marks Office and in other countries.

www.eHarlequin.com

Printed in U.S.A.

ABOUT THE AUTHOR

Ann Roth has always been a voracious reader of everything from classics to mysteries to romance. Of all the books she's read, love stories have affected her the most and stayed with her the longest. A firm believer in the power of love, Ann enjoys creating emotional stories that illustrate how love can triumph over seemingly insurmountable odds.

Ann lives in the greater Seattle area with her husband and a really irritating cat who expects her breakfast no later than 6:00 a.m., seven days a week.

She would love to hear from readers. You can write her c/o P.O. Box 25003, Seattle WA 98165-1903 or e-mail her at ann@annroth.net.

Books by Ann Roth

HARLEQUIN AMERICAN ROMANCE
1031—THE LAST TIME WE KISSED
1103—THE BABY INHERITANCE
1120—THE MAN SHE'LL MARRY

For Kathleen Scheibling. You have taught me so much. Thank you for believing in me.

Special thanks to my talented daughter, Kathryn Schuessler, for answering my many photography questions. Any errors are mine.

Chapter One

Dishes clattered and waitresses bustled back and forth, catering to the noon crowd that filled Rosy's Diner. Normally, Cammie Yarnell would've felt a tad smug that she'd snagged a booth. Today there were more important things on her mind. As she finished the last of her cranberry chicken salad, she shook her head at her lunch date. "I can't believe the girl I used to babysit is getting married."

"Believe it." Kelly Atwood beamed, the freckles on her cheeks seeming to dance. "I'm twenty-four—no girl anymore. Rick and I have been together since high school. It's about time we got married." She shrugged. "At least that's what Daddy says."

"Ah," Cammie said.

Weston Atwood, the local big shot, owned and ran the *Cranberry News Weekly*, the Oregon town's only newspaper. He also owned the local radio station and a chunk of prime real estate along the water of their seaside resort town. And bought all of his insurance through the company Cammie's parents owned and operated. Keeping him happy was important, but Kelly's happiness also mattered.

"Are you sure you want to get married?" Cammie probed, just to make certain Weston hadn't bullied his only child into something she wasn't ready for.

"Definitely." Kelly's shoulder-length brown hair swayed as she nodded. "I've dreamed of it since the first time Rick kissed me, back in eleventh grade."

Her eyes went all starry. Cammie suffered a wistful pang, which she quickly stifled. "Then I'm thrilled for you," she said, reaching across the table to squeeze Kelly's hand.

"That means a lot to me." Kelly smiled softly. "I owe you so much, Cammie. After Mom died, you were the only person I could talk to." Her eyes filled. "Sometimes you still are."

"I know, sweetie." Cammie's eyes filled, too, and she recalled ten-year-old Kelly falling apart in her then seventeen-year-old arms more than once. "I'm glad I was there for you."

After a moment of shared sniffles and watery smiles, Kelly swiped at her eyes and straightened. "Daddy, Rick and I want you to plan the wedding."

"I'd be insulted if you didn't." Cammie went into business mode, sliding her BlackBerry from her enormous leather bag, which doubled as purse and briefcase. "Have you set a date?"

"June seventh."

A push of the keypad and the month of June the following year appeared on the display. "It's good that you're booking early. I have a bar mitzvah May thirtieth and a wedding July twenty-sixth, but the seventh is wide open. Which happens to be a Sunday." She frowned at Kelly. "Did you know that?"

The young bride-to-be fiddled nervously with her napkin. "June seventh *this* year falls on a Saturday."

This year? "But that's only six weeks from now!" Cammie clapped her hand over her suddenly panicky heart, then eyed her younger friend. "You're not pregnant, are you?"

Flushing, Kelly shook her head. "Goodness, no. But Rick starts med school in August, and we want to get married and settled in Portland before then. I know this is short notice, but can you fit us in?"

Cammie pulled up May and June of this year. The second week in May was the eighth-grade graduation dance, a town tradition and rite of passage for kids before they started high school. There was nothing else scheduled until a wedding on June thirtieth. She could easily work in one more wedding.

"I'll do it," she said, "but with the tight time frame I may not be able to add the usual special touches to make your wedding day extra wonderful." Which seemed a shame. Another thought struck her. "And unfortunately my parents will be out of town until June eleventh." They were about to leave for a month-long trip to Europe, in celebration of their thirty-fifth anniversary. "Their tickets are nonrefundable and nonexchangeable. They'll be sick about missing this."

Kelly's face fell, but she nodded. "I understand, and so will Daddy. I contacted Fran Bishop, and she said we could have the wedding at the Oceanside Bed and Breakfast."

"Really?" *Oh, great.* Cammie rubbed the space between her eyes, where the faint pain signaling an impending stress headache had started.

On cue, "nosy Rosy" bustled over with the coffee-pot. "Refill, ladies?"

"Please," Cammie said. Though at this point she'd have preferred alcohol, she didn't drink in the afternoon.

"You okay?" the fiftysomething waitress/diner owner asked, scrutinizing her like a fish she might buy at the market.

"Actually, Kelly just shared some wonderful news." Arranging her expression into bland happiness, Cammie smiled fondly at her companion, who silently nodded her assent to share the information. "She and Rick are getting married."

Rosy lit up. "Congratulations, honey, and about time."

Then she gave Cammie the same quick, veiled look she used every time Cammie planned somebody else's wedding—friendly concern with a hint of compassion. But Cammie was fine. And tired of the woman's mis-placed pity. She really ought to find another place to eat and hold client meetings. Mentally she rolled her eyes. Physically she widened her grin, which seemed to mollify Rosy.

"You girls want dessert, to celebrate?" she asked as she deftly collected the dishes and juggled the coffee-pot. "I have a beautiful cheesecake, or some freshly made coconut cream pie." She looked at Kelly. "On the house in honor of your engagement."

Cammie's mouth watered, but since turning thirty last year her metabolism had slowed. Now everything she ate went straight to her hips. Which was why she and her best friend, Jules, had signed up to play coed volleyball starting next week. She shook her head. "Coffee is fine."

"Me, too," Kelly said. "But thanks. And feel free to spread the word about me and Rick," she added.

As if she needed to.

After the busybody hurried off, Kelly frowned. "The Oceanside's okay with you, right? I know that's where you and Todd were supposed to get married. And you haven't done a wedding there since…"

Chewing her lip and shredding her napkin, she looked worried half to death. Cammie hurried to reassure her.

"That was nearly a year ago. I'm over it now," she lied.

Not a day went by that she didn't yearn for what might have been. The cottage near the ocean she and Todd had looked into buying, possibly a baby on the way…

She silently chastised herself. The pity-party was getting old, especially since she now realized she'd loved the idea of getting married more than she'd loved Todd. And as her parents reassured her time and again, eventually she'd find the right somebody. She was thirty-one years old, which by her estimation gave her a good nine years to have the three children she wanted. But unless she got past what might have been and moved on, falling in love never would happen.

What better way to start fresh than to plan a wedding at the scene of the crime? "The Oceanside is perfect," she enthused. With its open floor plan, large rooms and oceanfront location, it truly was.

"Good, because Daddy loves the idea. And since he's the man with the checkbook…"

No need to finish that sentence. What Weston Atwood wanted, Weston Atwood got.

"You're sure June seventh is okay with Fran?" Cammie asked.

By then tourist season would be in full swing, and Fran's popular oceanfront bed-and-breakfast was sure to be packed. Without fail she cooked gourmet breakfasts and pampered her guests with wine and cheese socials every afternoon, keeping her busy and then some.

"She was thrilled at the idea," Kelly said. "Said her guests would love the idea of a wedding in the great room. Of course they'll be invited to the reception after the ceremony."

"In that case, we're on." Cammie extracted a yellow pad from her bag and laid it on the table. She reached into the inside pocket and retrieved her silver Waterman's pen, a gift of appreciation from the Pendeltons, repeat clients, after their fiftieth anniversary party last year. "Now, let's talk about what you and Rick—"

"Um, Cammie," Kelly interrupted, "there's something else you should know."

The anxious look on her face put Cammie on alert. "What's that?"

"You're not gonna like this." Kelly brought her cup to her lips then lowered it without sipping. After a few seconds of unbearable silence, she dropped her bomb. "Daddy hired Curt Blanco to photograph everything."

Curt Blanco. The very name grated against Cammie's nerves, and under the table her foot tapped rapidly on the black-and-white linoleum. The despicable man, whom she once had considered a close friend and often had worked with, was responsible for introducing her to Todd. Curt had watched her fall in love, never once bothering to mention that Todd was a liar and a cheat. Instead she'd discovered the ugly fact herself, the morning after the bachelor party.

Some friend Curt Blanco had turned out to be. She narrowed her eyes. "I no longer work with that man."

"I know, and I tried to change Daddy's mind, but he says Curt's the best and he won't settle for anyone else. Besides, Daddy says you two were the best event planner–photographer team on the west coast and it's time you moved past your personal problems and worked together again."

"Well, your daddy is wrong."

Now Cammie relied on other photographers. She and Curt barely glanced at each other, barely spoke when they met. Which, given that the population of Cranberry was only 2,274, happened regularly.

Then came the final question. "Does this mean you won't plan my wedding?"

Kelly was like family. She looked up to Cammie, and Cammie knew she couldn't let her down.

Besides, she and Curt were both professionals able to separate business from their personal lives. As long as she remembered that, she could handle working with him again. Just this once.

"Of course, I'll do it," she assured Kelly. Squaring her shoulders, she uncapped the Waterman's and poised it over her notepad. "Let's get started."

STANDING IN THE SPACIOUS, glass-walled great room of the Oceanside Bed and Breakfast, camera gear piled on the oversize armchair beside him, Curt Blanco shifted un-comfortably. Who wouldn't, when across the room Weston, Kelly and Rick sat hunched over the coffee table with Cammie Yarnell? They were hammering out wedding details and had been for a while now. Fran Bishop, who owned the place, had let them in, served refreshments and then disappeared into her basement apartment.

As gigs went, this one sucked big-time, and Curt wished he could disappear, too. But Weston Atwood signed his paycheck at the paper and recommended Curt to friends in need of a photographer, and Curt wasn't about to sabotage that relationship. Especially now, when his father's medical insurance had run out. Thanks to a nasty car accident, Curt and his brothers were strapped with bills for the old man's back and hip surgeries, plastic surgery and ongoing, extensive physical therapy.

No, he'd do the job and do it well. Which meant taking pictures from now through the wedding five weeks from now. Nothing digital. Weston wanted things done the old-fashioned way—film and the darkroom.

"Hey, Curt. You going to stand there all afternoon, or photograph us planning the big day?" Weston settled his portly frame in his easy chair. "I'm sick of grinning."

"Just waiting for you to relax," Curt said. "Forget I'm here and I'll take the candid photos you want."

Kelly nodded. Rick, whose family had hired Curt several times in the past, shrugged.

"You'll photograph me grinning or not at all," Weston ordered, slipping into his usual bulldog glare. He pointed a menacing finger at the camera and re-pasted the phony, jovial expression on his face.

Ignoring Curt, Cammie jotted something on her notepad. Except for the tightening of her lips, she might not have acknowledged him at all.

Nothing new there. Since she'd caught Todd in bed with two women and had called off her wedding, she'd avoided Curt as if he had a contagious disease.

Not that he gave a damn.

Right, and life is filled with happy endings.

Stifling a scowl, he selected a thirty-millimeter telephoto lens from the equipment bag. He caught Kelly, radiant as she beamed at her soon-to-be husband, and Rick, dazzled with love. A rare shot of Weston genuinely smiling at his daughter, his pleasure over the engagement evident. Then the camera found Cammie.

Five foot six, round in all the right places, blue-eyed, blond and smart to boot, she made his breath catch. He'd been hot for her since eighth grade, a secret he kept to himself.

Now she hated his guts.

Wincing, he manually focused his Leica. She'd always favored skirts. This one was pleated, deep green and short, and with her legs crossed, exposed a decent chunk of thigh. He zoomed in to the small bouquet of violets tattooed above her ankle, visible through her panty hose. They'd been together when she'd got that, high-school friends in search of identity. Cammie, who favored vivid colors, had fallen in love with the rich blue-purple color of violets. Curt had chosen a video camera on his calf because he'd known even then that photography was his future.

Her parents were strict and she'd been forced to hide the tattoo for a while. Not Curt. By then his mom had been sick and past caring at all about stuff like that. And the old man had been engrossed in his latest bimbo, who'd become the second of his four wives.

Curt narrowed the shot. *Click-click.* He grinned to

himself, knowing these photos were for him alone. Next he focused on Cammie's face, alive with excitement over some wedding detail. Damn, but she was beautiful.

And off-limits.

Suddenly, she noticed the camera. Her generous mouth flattened, her eyes narrowed and her back went as straight as a soldier's.

Curt didn't think he could handle five straight weeks of frost-queen attitude, not from Cammie. Time to thaw the ice for good. So what if he'd already tried with phone calls, letters and e-mails? She'd ignored them all. Never answered her door, either. But he'd stopped pestering her months ago, and didn't the experts talk about the healing power of time? Surely almost twelve months after the fact, working together on this wedding, she'd soften and they'd make up.

Why Curt wanted that so badly was beyond him. But he did, and if necessary he'd beg, borrow, grovel… Anything.

He offered a careful smile—not too warm, don't want to piss her off. For his effort he received a disapproving frown that made him feel two inches tall.

She still blamed him for the whole mess with Todd, when the fault lay with Todd. Yeah, the guy had been Curt's friend, but how was he supposed to know he couldn't keep his pants zipped?

The morning after Todd's bachelor party she'd caught him in bed with two strippers. Which sucked and hurt and turned out to be the last of a long line of sexual betrayals, but sure as hell wasn't Curt's fault.

Aiming out the floor-to-ceiling window, he snapped several photos of the ocean. The tide was coming in and frothy waves teased the sand, only to dart back, the way a hard-to-get woman might.

The group stood, and Curt pivoted toward them, focusing on Cammie, who stood like a sentry.

Under the cover of the camera, he let his gaze go where it wanted. It drifted from her short, blond hair, the natural curl tamed, to her chest, which, thanks to her rigid shoulders, stuck out. She wasn't stacked, but not small, either. Once, during the eighth-grade graduation dance, those breasts had pillowed against his chest when a spin-the-bottle game had paired them.

Curt shot a close-up of her face, her head held high on her long neck. It had been nearly seventeen years, but he still remembered standing in the closet with her that Friday night, excited, aroused and as scared as hell. His first ever kiss, though not hers, and the whole thing had just about knocked him off his feet. She'd smelled good, tasted like bubble gum, and he'd sprouted a giant erection. Certain he was in love, he'd floated through the rest of the weekend.

Not Cammie. Their school had housed grades one through twelve, and plenty of older guys had noticed and liked her. By Monday she and the freshman football quarterback had been going steady and she'd all but forgotten about Curt.

After licking his wounds and pretending he didn't care, he'd gotten involved with Joanie Bates, who was two years older and the fastest girl in school. She'd initiated him into the wonderful world of sex and he'd never looked back.

Weston moved toward the dining room, which was separated from the great room by a shoulder-high bookcase. He unlatched and slid open the glass door that opened onto a huge view deck and was adjacent to the dining-room table. "I want this open that night, so it feels like we're on the ocean."

The scent of chill, salt air gusted into the room, momentarily overpowering the aromas of coffee and fresh-baked cookies Fran had supplied.

"Weather-wise, June is fickle," Cammie reminded him. "It's bound to be chilly, and could rain. You don't want to freeze your guests." She gestured at the windows. "The panoramic view you want is right there."

Scoffing, Weston dismissed the concern. "That's what heaters are for, sweetheart."

A nickname she detested. Watching her closely, Curt waited for her to let Weston know. She never got the chance.

Paying her no attention at all, the businessman pushed on with his own agenda. "We ought to have fireworks. Can you pull that off, Cammie? I'll pay whatever it costs."

Rick and Kelly shared alarmed glances. "No disrespect meant, sir," Rick began, "but Kelly and I don't want fireworks."

"Nonsense, son. We'll have 'em, and you'll be glad we did. Got that, Cammie?"

"I'll look into it," she said, jotting a note on her pad, "but I really think we should make this the wedding Kelly and Rick want."

Weston Atwood's steely gray eyes glinted. "I'm not paying you to think, sweetheart."

"Daddy!" Kelly scolded.

Her father scowled at her. "Look, I'm the one with the brains. Cammie knows that, and so do you."

Cammie opened her mouth, but Curt cut in, his first opportunity to get back into her good graces. "She's not your sweetheart, and you know damned well she's smart. That's why people pay her big bucks to think and create."

Cutting past the shocked look on Weston's face—Curt had never spoken to his boss that way—he turned to Cammie. Instead of a grateful smile, her eyes widened and shot him a be-quiet look.

So much for getting on her good side.

He waited uneasily for Weston to fire him and wondered how he'd pay his share of his dad's medical bills.

Kelly looked surprised and impressed, and Rick seemed downright amazed. Why couldn't Cammie feel like that?

Because she was impossibly stubborn, and not about to forgive him. Not yet.

Several moments passed but Weston didn't react to Curt's outburst. Casually, Curt grabbed a cookie from the plate Fran had set on the dining-room table and chewed without tasting. His friends didn't call him Curt the Rock for nothing. He was just as stubborn, and he'd always liked challenges.

He and Cammie would be friends again, and if it took the whole five weeks to convince her, so be it.

NOBODY TALKED BACK to Weston Atwood, yet Curt had. Admiration filled Cammie before she remembered—this was *Curt* and she was still angry at him. Never mind his charming smile and warm eyes. She refused to be charmed or warmed, and raised her chin to prove it.

"I'd like a private word with my daughter and future son-in-law." Weston jerked his double chin toward the deck. "Outside."

"Of course," Cammie soothed, stepping out of his way. She hoped Kelly's father didn't strong-arm her and Rick into doing something they didn't want to do. "While you do that, I'll take some measurements."

"I'll keep you company," Curt added with a challenging look.

The last thing Cammie wanted was to be alone with the man, but she didn't have much choice. "Suit yourself," she muttered.

"I'll deal with you later," Weston warned Curt as he closed the glass door behind himself, Kelly and Rick.

Curt seemed unfazed. He was like that—burying his feelings under feigned nonchalance—and had been since his mother had died when he was nineteen. Though once, while she'd been sick, he *had* broken down in tears. At the time, he and Cammie had been close friends, and she knew he'd been mortified by the show of feelings. That never had happened again. Every woman he'd dated, and there'd been dozens, wanted to unlock that emotional core. None had succeeded.

Now he stood beside the dining-room table chewing his oatmeal-raisin cookie. Which smelled heavenly and made Cammie's stomach rumble.

Refusing to bow to temptation she moved around the table to the serving counter that separated the dining room and kitchen. She set down her bag and dug into it for the tape measure. Even though her head was bent, she felt Curt staring at her.

Jerking up, she glared at him. "What is your problem?"

He had the gall to look hurt, his hangdog expression reminding her of a lost puppy.

She felt bad for snapping at him. In a weak moment she moved closer, reached up and swiped a cookie crumb from the corner of his mouth. The glint of heat in his eyes totally unnerved her.

Had she lost her mind? She tried to retract her hand, but Curt caught hold of her, lacing her fingers with his. His hand was large and warm against her cold skin.

"I stood up to Weston for you," he said, rubbing his thumb over hers. "I could lose my job. Aren't you going to thank me?"

She hadn't been touched in a long time, and his solid grip felt disturbingly good. "I'm perfectly capable of defending myself, thank you very much."

"You're welcome anyway."

With his mouth quirked and his brown eyes teasing, he was irresistible, damn him. His thumb continued to rub lazy circles over her hand. Heat eddied through her. Her body tilted toward him before her thoughts stopped her. *For goodness' sake, this is Curt!*

Cammie stiffened. "Let go of me."

The shocked look on his face—caused by her words or the fact that he was touching her like a lover—assured her that he'd meant no harm. He dropped her hand as if it burned and backed away.

Turning her back on him, she marched into the great room to continue with her work.

"When are you going to get that stick out of your butt and start being nice to me again?" he said.

"Stick up my…?" She whirled toward him. "What do you expect? I don't trust you anymore. I never will."

Though his neutral expression never changed, he blinked solemnly. Cammie knew she'd hurt him.

"I'm sorry about what Todd pulled," he said in a quiet, careful voice, "but as I keep trying to tell you, I had nothing to do with it."

"You could have warned me." And she should have been more tuned in to the smooth-talking male who'd swept her off her feet with ardent attention and declarations of love, all the while sleeping with other women. She still felt stupid about her naiveté. Why hadn't she realized what a player Todd was?

"Believe me, I didn't know he was a jerk until you did," Curt said. "Like at any bachelor party, those strippers were just for kicks. I never figured he'd sleep with them, and I swear, I knew nothing about the others, either. Fooling around on you was Todd's best-kept secret."

He looked squarely into her eyes. "Be thankful you found out before the wedding. If you'd married Todd and *then* learned he was fooling around on you…" He shook his head.

Curt's father had done exactly that to his mother, just before she'd been diagnosed with cancer. The divorce had torn apart the family, and the legal and medical bills had hurtled them into bankruptcy.

"I suppose you're right," she conceded.

He shot her a careful look. "Does this mean you forgive me at long last?"

For a few moments she imagined renewing their easy friendship. A tight place deep inside her eased. But Curt was from the past, which was behind her. Besides, over the last eleven-plus months, she'd gotten along fine without him. And no matter what he said, she couldn't quite trust him.

"Too much has happened and we can't go back," she said. "I don't want to be friends." The sudden, empty feeling inside was from hunger, she was sure.

"Maybe you'll change your mind?"

"Don't count on it. You know me, Curt. Once I make up my mind, that's that."

A challenging gleam flared in his eyes, and for a moment she thought he'd argue. But his expression registered resignation.

"If that's what you want." He reached for another cookie.

He'd given up so easily. Was their friendship—was *she*—that insignificant to him? That hurt, which, since the decision to move on was hers, was utterly confusing.

Cammie pasted a cool, casual smile on her face. "That's exactly what I want."

Chapter Two

Thursday night Curt trudged into the dingy Cranberry Grade and High School boys' locker room along with his two older brothers and two dozen twenty-, thirty- and fortysomething males. He hadn't been here in thirteen years, since he'd played center for the varsity basketball team his senior year.

The familiar smell of unwashed socks and stale air permeated the room.

After a long day, he wanted to go home and relax, but his brothers had strong-armed him. Absently registering the usual locker-room jokes, he toed out of his wingtips.

As he changed into gym shorts and a T-shirt, he frowned at Eric and Steven, who were doing the same. "Tell me again why you dragged my butt here?"

Eric shrugged. "The article in the paper said the volleyball league needs players, and you don't have to be a superjock to join. Plus, we're not getting any younger. We all could use the exercise."

Curt glanced at his brother's flat abs and shook his head. "You manage two cranberry bogs. You get plenty of exercise."

"Maybe he does, but you and I don't get near enough," Steven, who was a local DJ, pointed out. Which wasn't true, since he played baseball and basketball, and sometimes jogged with Curt. "But the main reason is this is a *coed* league." He winked. "A good place to meet babes."

"We already know most of the women in Cranberry," Curt argued. "Hell, between the three of us, we've dated a fair number of 'em." He jerked his T-shirt over his head. "Women are a pain, and I'm not in the mood to deal with any new ones."

Steven rolled his eyes. "Then for Pete's sake, hook up with somebody you know, 'cause you need to get laid. Tonight."

"That's your answer to everything." Eric scoffed as he stepped into his gym shorts. "And the reason you've been divorced twice at thirty-four."

"Yeah, well you've been divorced, too." Steven plopped onto the scarred bench and shoved his big feet into his sneakers. "And you're thirty-two."

Eyes narrowed, Eric dropped down beside him. "Well, I'm married now. The only reason Kit didn't invite you guys over for dinner tonight is she's pulling a double shift at the library. Believe me, I'm a contented man."

"So far. It's only been a year." Steven glanced at Curt, who was hunkered down, double-lacing his sneakers. "Wanna bet he'll get tired of Kit before long?"

Eric's face darkened. "Like I keep telling you, I really love her. Our marriage is for keeps. So shut your trap."

The two brothers glared at each other as they stood, then directed twin stony gazes at Curt, the odd man out. They wanted him to weigh in. Short attention spans and

multiple divorces ran in the family, but after dating for
two years and a year of marriage, Eric and Kit were still
wild for each other. Maybe they'd make it, a first for any
Blanco male.

"You never know." He shrugged. "I'm with Eric on
this one." He aimed a somber look at his married brother.
"Now don't go proving me wrong."

"Curt sides with me. Yes!" Eric pumped his fist toward the ceiling.

"Yeah, but he's not himself," Steven said. "He hasn't
cracked a smile all night."

"What the hell are you talking about? I'm okay." As
Curt shoved his clothes and shoes into a locker, he
forced a smile that fooled nobody.

Bickering forgotten, his brothers shared a knowing
look. "Maybe he *does* need to get laid," Eric conceded.

"Screw the both of you." Curt slammed his locker shut.

Several men jerked surprised glances his way.

"Not us," Steven joked. "Some babe."

Laughter filled the room.

Curt's brothers meant well, and he figured they'd
drop the subject if he didn't react, so he bit back a pithy
reply and managed a good-natured grin. The other men
in the room went back to changing.

Considering he hadn't been with a woman in months,
he *should* want sex. He didn't though. Maybe he was
sick or something, or he'd been working too hard.

For some reason, he thought of Cammie. He frowned.
She had nothing to do with his AWOL sex drive. But everything to do with his rotten mood.

Turning his back on his brothers, he rested his palms
on the cinder block wall and stretched his hamstrings.

During the nearly twelve months since Cammie and Todd had gone their separate ways and Todd had left town, Curt had carried the hope that he and Cammie would resume what had been an enjoyable friendship. Until two days ago at the Oceanside.

She claimed to believe him now, finally accepting that he'd known nothing about Todd sleeping around. A huge relief that should have reopened the door to their friendship. Instead she'd locked that door and tossed away the key.

She didn't want to be friends. Period.

Bleak as that was, he wasn't ready to give up. This weekend kicked off the first of the parties, showers and dinners for Kelly and Rick, each occasion requiring Curt's services. As the party and wedding organizer, Cammie would be right there with him, and he planned to work on her at each event. Sooner or later she'd realize he wasn't going away and would let him back into her life.

In his mind he saw her, head high, posture straight, skin smooth and creamy. Even with her mouth tightly pursed and eyes shooting darts at him, she was beautiful. His blood stirred.

Get real. She wasn't attracted to him and never had been. Besides, what he wanted was her friendship.

As for the physical stuff… He had to do something to lift his spirits. May as well take his brothers' advice and hook up with someone tonight.

Men were filing out the exit leading to the gym. Curt nodded at his brothers. "Let's get out there and check out some women. Oh, and play volleyball."

"Atta boy." Eric grinned, and Steven threw him a thumbs-up.

"TELL ME AGAIN WHY WE'RE DOING this?" Cammie asked her best friend, Jules, as they and a dozen other women suited up in the Cranberry Grade and High School girls' locker room.

"For the exercise, and because the article in the paper said that the league needs more women," Jules said. She glanced at the attractive females in various states of undress, then leaned in and lowered her voice. "And because there are lots of cute, single men in the league."

A vision of Curt, tall and solid, brown eyes warm and mouth quirking, popped into Cammie's mind. Over the past few days she'd thought about him a lot more than she ever had before, in a whole different way. For the first time ever, she was physically attracted to him. Which, given that the man never had been more than a friend and was less than that now, was both troubling and weird.

Even more disturbing was her dream last night. The way his hands and mouth had touched her… Well, the whole thing had been extremely erotic. The memory of it brought a hot flush to her face.

Jules peered at her in alarm. "You're all red. Are you coming down with something?"

"I'm fine," Cammie assured her. Just a little sex deprived.

Her hearty tone didn't work. Jules continued to study her with concern. "You said you were over Todd and ready to move forward. Tonight you could meet your Mr. Right. Unless…" Frown lines formed between her eyebrows. "You're not backing out of this, are you?"

Cammie shook her head. "I'm thirty-one years old. My biological clock won't run forever. I'm moving on with my life, starting now." Her attraction for Curt and

that titillating dream were simply the result of not having a steady man in her life. "But the main reason I'm
here tonight is for the exercise."

Jules sighed with relief. "That's the spirit. I need
exercise, too, but there's nothing wrong with checking
out the men while we chase the volleyball. Who knows,
you could meet a great guy here."

Moving to the mirror, she freshened her peach-color
lipstick, while Janey Jones and Marcy Docker, two attractive twentysomething acquaintances, fixed their
ponytails and checked their makeup.

Cammie joined them. She caught Janey's eye in the
mirror. "Have you two played before?"

"This is our second year," Janey said.

"Really?" Both younger women looked trim and fit,
which worried Cammie. She bit her lip. "Do you have
to be good at volleyball? Because I'm not. I don't even
know if I'll qualify to play."

"No problem," Marcy said. "The really competitive
types play someplace else. For this league, you don't
even have to try out."

Janey nodded. "Team members are selected randomly
by computer and grouped with team captains, who are
experienced, but laid-back players. Once they put us in
groups, we choose team names and then practice, some
of us in the gym, some at the soccer field behind the gym,
and the rest at the baseball park next door."

"We rotate locations every Tuesday and Thursday,"
Marcy added.

"Right," Janey said. "If the school needs the gym, we
use the field behind Town Hall. Practice and games start

at 7:30 and end by 10:00." She leaned toward the mirror to freshen her mascara. "That's how it works."

"Don't forget the best part," Marcy said. "After we shower and clean up, some of us head out for beer. It's the same routine—practice or games and then go out and relax—every time. A real hoot."

Exactly what Cammie needed to hear. Reassured, she nodded.

"Am I right about the men?" Jules asked, raising her eyebrows. "Did you meet anyone new and interesting last year?"

"You mean, somebody we don't already know?" Marcy shook her head. "No, but we both ended up dating guys we'd never really talked to until we joined the league."

"The single men and the fun are why we're here for another season," Janey said.

"Music to my ears." Jules grinned and tugged at her baby-blue, formfitting Lycra outfit, which showed off her smooth, trim body. "That's also why we're here."

Unlike Jules, Cammie was too lumpy for anything but longish gym shorts and a loose tank top. She shot her friend an envious look. "I wish I were in better shape."

"Men love your body," Jules said. "I'd sure like some of your curves."

As Cammie smoothed her hair, her thoughts again turned to Curt. He thought she looked good, or so he'd said back when they were friends. But he hadn't seen her in gym clothes since high school. What would he think of her now? Not that he'd ever see her dressed like this. Thank goodness. If he did, though…

What was the matter with her, thinking about *him* again? She frowned. Working with him was going to be a real pain, exacerbated by this new and unwanted sexual attraction.

The best way to get past that was to find a new love interest. May as well start looking tonight. She borrowed Jules's lipstick, which suited her fair skin and almost matched her outfit.

"Well, then." With a critical eye on her profile, she sucked in her stomach, tugged down her tank top and nodded. "Let's go check out the guys." She glanced at Janey and Marcy, who wore twin grins. "And, um, play volleyball."

As THE EIGHT TEAM CAPTAINS took turns calling out the names of their team members, Curt barely heard. How could he concentrate, with Cammie standing across the gym?

The Cammie he knew liked to walk on the beach. She wasn't much for competitive sports. What was she doing here?

Beside him, Steven murmured, "Will you look at Jules Workman. What a babe."

Curt checked out Cammie instead. Wearing pink gym shorts that showed off her shapely legs and a matching tank top that emphasized her round breasts, she looked hot.

"Is she dating anybody?" Steven asked.

"How should I know? I came here to play volleyball."

"Jeez, Curt, lighten up."

Curt decided to do just that. No point in letting Cammie ruin his fun. He was here to have fun and scout out women, and he would. "Jules likes men who play hard to get," he cautioned.

The words earned him a sideways look from Eric and a curious frown from Steven. "Where'd you hear that?"

"Cammie." Back when they were friends, Curt had often heard about Jules's boyfriends, who came and went through a never-ending revolving door. A real heartbreaker, she never stayed with one guy for long. Exactly the right challenge for Steven.

"Cammie's looking great, too," Steven noted.

Eric shot Curt a curious look. "You two made up yet?"

"Nope," he said, sounding grouchy to his own ears.

"You always did have a thing for her," Eric observed in his wise older-brother tone. "Why not go after her and see what happens?"

"Curt Blanco," called out Mike Anderson, one of the team captains.

"See ya." Curt trotted over to the two teammates named so far—sexy Marcy Docker and Billy Seddles, the town stud and a good athlete. With him on the team, they'd do well.

Cammie was standing with the thirty or so as-yet-to-be-called, playing the social game that came so easily to her. Drawn by her beauty and bubbly conversation, men and women clustered around her.

Suddenly she noticed Curt. The smile on her face faded and her eyes narrowed a fraction. For sure, she wasn't happy to see him.

Damn, he hated that. He matched her mood with a sober nod and vowed again to somehow coax her back into friendship. She turned away as if she didn't know him and his morale plummeted.

He greeted his teammates. Mike, busy with the roster, stood to one side. Billy and Marcy gestured him over.

"There are some fine-looking women here tonight," Billy said, licking his lips.

The guy was a bed-'em and dump-'em, first-class jerk. No brain surgeon, either. He worked in receiving at the employee-owned cranberry factory and didn't earn much, yet women seemed to like him. Must be the muscles and cleft chin.

"I'm fine, too." Marcy shaped her plump mouth into an attractive pout. "Hello, Curt, and welcome to our team," she purred, linking her arm through his.

Big eyes, big breasts, small waist, and long legs— definitely sweet stuff. She smelled good, too. Exactly what he liked.

She was practically drooling, and her warm breast pressed invitingly against his biceps. Yet beyond mild interest, he felt nothing.

What was his problem?

"Glad to be on your team," he said, forcing a smile as he untangled himself. He glanced at Cammie, eyeing him with cool indifference, and amped up his grin. "You're lookin' good tonight, Marcy."

"I'm a darned good volleyball player, too," she cooed.

"Looks and skill. Great combo," Billy drawled. Then he nodded at Cammie. "Get a load of Cammie Yarnell. I always liked blondes."

Knowing she'd never give the pea-brained bum the time of day, Curt snickered. "She's not your type, and for sure she'd never be interested in you."

"Yeah, well she *looks* interested."

Damned if it wasn't true. Her eyelids lowered seductively and her cheeks flushed a pretty pink. Then her lips curled into a teasing, seductive smile that confused

Curt—he'd never seen her flirt like that—and caused
Billy to whistle under his breath.

"She dating anybody?"

Curt didn't think so. What she needed was a man who
wouldn't fool around on her, who wanted kids and a
house with a picket fence. A sleaze like Billy would just
waste her time. He scowled. "Stay away from her."

Both Billy and Mary shot him surprised looks.

"You got a thing for her?" Billy asked.

Curt shook his head. "Hell, no."

"Cammie Yarnell," Mike called out.

Well, well. She was on their team. Curt crossed his
arms. This should be interesting, and would give him
more time to get back on her good side. He watched her
move reluctantly toward his group, and frowned when
she smiled at Billy.

"Yes!" The ladies' man shot his fist skyward. "I'm
gonna ask her to share a pitcher after practice tonight."
He glanced Curt's way. "If you're okay with that."

He wasn't, but he shrugged.

"Maybe we could double date," Marcy said, literally
batting her lashes.

Drinking a beer at home in front of the tube sounded
better, but Cammie needed protecting.

Curt forced a smile. "Why not?"

Chapter Three

Sitting in the dim light of the Cranberry Bar and Grill with Billy Seddles, Cammie sipped her red wine and pretended to have a good time. While she felt great after a few hours of exercise and a refreshing shower, she'd had enough socializing for one night. Country-and-western music vibrated through the room, so loud that conversation was virtually impossible except between songs. If this was the "hoot" Marcy had referred to in the locker room earlier tonight, Cammie wanted no part of it. Not with Billy, anyway. Though good-looking, the man was as dumb as a volleyball, and as likely to stray as a tomcat, which made him worthless as husband material.

So what was she doing, sharing a booth with him, Curt and party-girl Marcy?

Curt and Marcy. The very idea of those two together rankled. From under lowered lashes, Cammie glanced at them across the table. Marcy was draped all over Curt, and though he wasn't exactly salivating, he didn't seem to mind, either.

And to think, she'd actually liked Marcy in the locker room. The empty-headed flirt was all wrong for Curt!

Couldn't he see that? Of course not. All he cared about was the cleavage revealed by her low-cut, skintight, chartreuse belly shirt.

Men!

Biting back the urge to kick him under the table, Cammie crossed her ankles and compressed her lips.

As if he heard her brain scolding him, Curt aimed a questioning look at her. Since what he did and whom he did it with were none of Cammie's concern, she banished her disapproval.

Striving to appear intrigued with Billy, she leaned toward him. "You picked a great name for our team," she praised. "The Big Time Players sounds so…"

"Clever," Marcy finished, cuddling closer to Curt.

"Clever—that's me." Billy preened and dropped his arm around Cammie's shoulders. She wanted to move away, but with Curt staring, she instead widened her eyes and smiled.

Curt shook off Marcy. "I'm tired of waiting for the waitress," he said over the music. "I'll get us a new pitcher." He grabbed the empty one and stood.

The music stopped. "Get Cammie another wine, too," Billy said.

She'd already downed two glasses in quick succession and felt slightly drunk. Any more and she wouldn't be able to drive home. Jules would be no help, for she and Steven Blanco had headed to Rosy's for a quiet, late-night meal alone—an interesting development Cammie couldn't wait to hear about. She opened her mouth to decline the offer of more alcohol, but Curt cut her off.

"She's had enough."

"What are you, my guardian angel?" Cammie frowned and promptly changed her mind. "I happen to want another glass."

Billy's arm tightened around her shoulders. "You heard the lady."

Curt's eyes narrowed and his mouth formed a thin line, and she thought he might hit the other man. But he released a breath and shrugged one shoulder. "Whatever."

She watched him amble to the bar, his long stride a pleasure to watch. He always had looked good in jeans, and his navy T-shirt showed off his broad back.

"What are you lookin' at him for, when you got me?" Billy queried in a low, seductive voice.

Cammie locked gazes with Marcy, who rolled her eyes.

The oblivious male grinned, exposing large, white teeth. "Women like to sleep with me, and you know why? I have a long tongue, and I know how to use it." He stuck it out, wiggled it and touched it to his nose.

Ugh, Cammie thought, pulling out of his grasp. But Marcy squirmed in her seat and made a soft, throaty sound of approval.

"Amazing," she enthused, leaning forward.

Billy stared openly at her Wonderbra cleavage and inched away from Cammie.

A toe-tapping song that wasn't as loud as before started on the jukebox. "Would you like to dance?" he asked Marcy.

The younger woman glanced at Cammie. "But you're with Cammie."

"We're just friends," Cammie assured her. And hardly that. "You two go ahead."

The couple headed happily for the dance floor, passing Curt on the way.

He reached the booth and slid into the bench across from Cammie. "What a jackass," he said, frowning at Billy. "Why did you come here with him?"

To keep an eye on you and Marcy. "Because he invited me. I can't believe you showed up tonight. Are you stalking me?"

Anger flared in his eyes. "That hurts, Cammie. I had no idea you signed up to play volleyball. You don't seem like the sporty type."

Which was true. Contrite, she bit her lip. "I know you wouldn't stalk me. That was rude, and I apologize."

"Accepted. Are you interested in Billy?" Curt asked, his expression guarded.

"No," Cammie said, and the tension ebbed from his face. "But Marcy is."

"So I noticed."

The music stopped, and they sipped their drinks in more-or-less companionable silence. Moments later a sultry jazz tune sizzled from the jukebox. Billy and Marcy melded together.

"They're perfect for each other, aren't they?" Cammie observed.

"Amazing they didn't get together sooner," Curt replied, his gaze on the couple. He turned toward Cammie. "The question of the evening is, will they end up at Marcy's place or Billy's?"

The quirk of his lips and teasing glint in his eye made him look like a sexy-as-sin bad boy. Heat pulsed through Cammie's body. Not a good thing at all. Head buzzing from too much wine and strong, unwanted attraction for

Curt, she dropped her eyes to her glass, which was half-empty. She hadn't meant to drink the wine so quickly. "I don't know, but I'm sure we'll hear all about it at practice Tuesday night. What do you think about Jules and Steven?"

"That my brother finally met his match."

"Same goes for Jules. This ought to be interesting."

"My thoughts exactly. Want to bet on what happens?" Curt said, sounding like his old self.

Cammie smiled. "Jules will get tired of him and break his heart, just as she always does."

"Could be. I hear your parents are headed to Europe for a month."

That Curt knew about their trip came as no surprise. They'd been talking about it forever. Cammie nodded. "For their thirty-fifth wedding anniversary. I'll be driving them to the Portland airport bright and early Saturday morning. They'll miss Kelly's wedding, but with non-exchangeable, nonrefundable tickets…" That was the only glitch in their excitement. Weston Atwood was a major client, and they hated to miss his only child's wedding.

"It's about time they took a real vacation," Curt said. "Even Weston knows that."

Which was true. Her hardworking parents hadn't taken more than a few days off in ages. "Even so, they don't want to slight Weston or Kelly," Cammie said.

"An expensive gift ought to ease the pain." Curt tipped his glass toward her. "Here's to them."

Cammie did the same and they both sipped. They hadn't talked so comfortably in what seemed forever. She'd missed this, she realized. Why weren't they friends anymore? Trying to remember, she frowned.

"What made you sign up for volleyball?" Curt asked.

"I need the exercise." She gestured at her hips, hidden by the table.

His avid gaze traveled over her face, her breasts and up again, to her lips. "You look great to me."

The words and the warmth in his eyes pleased her way too much. He looked wonderful to her, too, and suddenly she wanted to show him exactly how wonderful. Luckily the table was between them. Otherwise she'd have twined her arms around his neck and kissed him.

A crazy and very bad idea. She shook her head. *Never should've drunk that third glass of wine.* "I heard about your father's car accident," she said. "I'm sorry."

His face sobered. "It's been a rough six months. He's had several surgeries and a world of pain that seems to be ongoing. Then there's the physical therapy. Big bucks for the medical people." He rubbed his thumb and other fingers together.

"That's what insurance is for," Cammie said. Since her parents sold the stuff, she ought to know.

"Unfortunately his ran out. My brothers and I are paying Dad's bills. That's why I need this wedding gig."

Cammie remembered when Curt's mother had run through her insurance when she'd been sick and in the middle of a divorce, and the bills and eventual bankruptcy that had plagued the family. "In that case, it's a good thing Weston hired you."

"As long as I keep my opinions to myself. When I stuck up for you the other day, I thought for sure he'd fire me, both from doing Kelly's wedding and the paper."

"He wouldn't fire you for that," she said.

"He's done it to others. Cross him and you're out."

Cammie's jaw dropped. "If that happened, you could sue and win."

"Not with his clout and posse of lawyers. Nope, what Weston wants, Weston gets." His eyes widened innocently. "I could have lost my paycheck for you."

If he was trying to charm her, he was doing it. Cammie rolled her eyes. "You're sure trying hard to get mileage from that."

"You bet I am. Since you didn't defend yourself, someone had to."

"I kept quiet because I want everything surrounding Kelly's wedding to be fun and happy. The best way to do that is to keep her daddy happy. If that means letting him say things to me that he shouldn't, so be it."

Curt scratched the back of his neck. "In other words, keep my mouth shut?"

"I'd appreciate that."

"Since I want to hold onto my job, okay."

He smiled and her heart flip-flopped. She wanted more than ever to kiss him. Instead she raised her glass. "Let's drink to zipping our lips."

As she drained her glass, she pictured herself and Curt with zippers on their mouths. That was so funny, she giggled. *That* set off a gale of laughter that had her swiping mirthful tears from her eyes.

"You're smashed." He looked concerned.

She didn't want concern. What she wanted was smoldering looks, hot kisses and... Enough!

"I'm okay." She rose, swaying slightly. "Time to go." Before she made a complete fool of herself.

"You're in no shape to drive." Curt stood. "I'll take you home."

He caught Billy's eye and gestured his chin toward the door. Billy nodded, then nuzzled Marcy's neck.

Before Cammie knew what was happening, she was buckled into Curt's CR-V, sailing down the road.

TWENTY MINUTES AFTER LEAVING the tavern, Curt pulled into Cammie's drive. The yellow porch light illuminated the door and front stoop of her small, neat bungalow, while softer light peeked through a crack in the living-room drapes. She always left on a light when she went out.

Curt glanced at her. With her head turned toward the window, he couldn't see her face. He touched her shoulder, which was warm and relaxed. "Wake up, Cammie. You're home."

"Okay." Releasing a sigh, she rolled her head his way.

Hair sticking out, eyes glazed with sleep, she looked sexy as hell. Curt imagined waking up beside her in the morning and his body went hard.

Was he nuts? This was Cammie, the woman who barely tolerated him. All he wanted was friendship. With the Blanco genes for fickleness, that was the most honest emotion he was capable of.

He jumped from the car. Cammie, who usually insisted on opening doors herself, waited for him to help her out. Boy, was she snockered.

She held his arm as he escorted her the twenty feet to the front door, but stood on her own to dig through her enormous purse for the key.

"Darn it, I can't find my key. Here," she said, handing him a paperback book, her BlackBerry, a plastic sack containing her gym clothes and a makeup bag.

More pawing, but no luck.

"Check the inside pocket," he suggested. Which was where she always carried it.

Nodding, she slipped her hand into the pocket, emerging with the key.

"Hooray," she said, flashing it and a triumphant smile.

She slung the purse over her shoulder. As she wheeled toward the door, Curt stuffed her things back into the bag, which bumped her waist.

And earned him a frown. "Are you making a pass at me?"

Though he wanted to do just that, he shook his head. "At you? Never."

"Oh," she said, sounding almost disappointed.

Wishful—no, insane—thinking, he decided.

She worked the key into the lock and finally the door opened. At last he could leave, before he turned himself into a liar and kissed her. The very thought pushed an unsteady breath from his lips.

"Good night, Cammie." He backed away—or tried.

"Wait." She grabbed his forearm.

Through his denim jacket he felt the warmth of her fingers. "What?" he growled.

Oblivious to his menacing tone, she looped her arms around his neck. "Thanks for bringing me home," she whispered.

Her leather blazer was unbuttoned and her breasts pressed sweetly against his chest. She smelled of lily-of-the-valley perfume, her longtime favorite, and she felt so damn good.

"What the hell are you doing?" Against his better judgment, he wrapped his arms around her.

"Thanking you," she said.

Only a fool would miss the desire in her eyes. A certain part of Curt's body stirred and began to rise. "You don't want to do this," he managed to say through gritted teeth.

"Yes, I do."

Her eyes pleaded and her mouth beckoned irresistibly, and he almost crumbled. Somehow he found the strength to stop holding her and disengage her arms. "You're already mad at me. I don't want you to hate me tomorrow," he said as he gently pushed her through the door.

She blinked as if suddenly remembering how she really felt about him. "You're right," she said, her face red with embarrassment. "I shouldn't have drunk all that wine."

He'd tried to stop her, but wisely kept that comment to himself. "You want to talk about this?"

She shook her head. "I'd rather forget the whole thing."

"Good idea," he said, doubtful that he would.

A relieved expression erased the pucker between her brows. "Thanks, Curt."

He wasn't sure what she was thanking him for, but hope stirred in his chest. "Does this mean we're friends again?"

Seconds passed while she silently scrutinized him, her face for once unreadable. "I honestly don't know."

Not exactly what he wanted to hear, but a definite improvement. He nodded.

"Good night, Curt."

"See you Saturday night." At the first engagement party for Kelly and Rick, choreographed by Cammie and photographed by him.

She muttered what sounded like "Yeah, great." The door closed with a firm click.

"WHAT HAPPENED WITH STEVEN?" Cammie asked when she phoned Jules the following morning.

"Hold on a sec while I tell Cinnamon something." Jules, who a year ago had been hired to run the human resources department at the cranberry factory, covered the mouthpiece.

Cinnamon Mahoney was her boss and the reason she had this job. A friend of Fran Bishop's, Cinnamon had come to Cranberry for a visit, staying at the Oceanside. Only instead of leaving, she'd ended up marrying Nick Mahoney, an inventor and handyman. She'd also saved the cranberry factory from shutting down by taking over as general manager and leading a successful employee-buyout program.

Cammie worked from home, a good thing, since she'd slept in this morning and was still wearing her pajamas and a pair of warm, fuzzy socks. Now, sitting at the kitchen table, she was halfway through her first cup of coffee, which wasn't jolting her awake as it usually did. Though it did drown out the sour taste of last night's wine....

"Sorry about that," Jules said. "You asked about Steven." Her voice lowered. "Nothing happened. He was a perfect gentleman, the cad." She sighed with disappointment. "Not even a kiss."

Curt hadn't kissed Cammie last night, either. Thank goodness. Recalling the way she'd thrown herself at him, she cringed. But that was too humiliating to share, and this conversation was about Jules.

"Cammie? Are you still there?"

"Just mulling over Steven's unusual behavior." She noticed a spot on her Mary Engelbreit place mat and made a mental note to toss it into the laundry. "Maybe he's not interested."

Curt wasn't interested in her, either, except as a friend. She didn't even want his friendship, let alone more. *Actions speak louder than words,* her mother always said. So that almost-kiss meant... Unable to go there, Cammie concentrated on Jules.

"Oh, Steven's interested, all right," Jules said. "I invited him to dinner tomorrow night, and he couldn't say 'what time' fast enough."

A thoroughly modern woman, Jules had no problem asking men out. Supporting her cheek with her fist, Cammie smiled. "Where are you taking him?"

"We're eating in, at my place. I'm making that goulash-stew recipe my grandpa taught me, the one he swore won my gram's heart."

Cammie couldn't mask her surprise. "But you don't cook." She didn't either, not since the breakup with Todd. But since she was moving on... She glanced at the shelf of neglected cookbooks above the stove and silently vowed to cook herself a from-scratch meal tonight. "You must really like Steven."

"I'm wild for him."

"But you barely know the man."

"My heart doesn't care. Besides, I know enough. Steven Blanco is one special guy."

"Are you sure this is Jules Workman?" Cammie teased.

Laughter filled her ear. "I can't believe myself, either."

"You know his reputation. Be careful."

"Not if I can help it." Cammie pictured her friend offering a sly wink. "Now, tell me about your night. What happened with Billy?"

"Marcy took him off my hands."

"But I thought she and Curt were together?"

"They started out that way, but she liked Billy better. He felt the same. They went home together, I think."

"You think?"

Cammie wished she'd left off those last two words. This could get embarrassing. "Um, we left before they did," she said, hoping Jules wouldn't pick up on the *we* part.

"We?"

No way to dodge that, so she told the truth. "Curt and I."

"Get out!" By the sound of her voice, Jules had leaned in closer to the phone. "I want details. Now."

Cammie frowned at her friend's enthusiasm. "It was nothing," she stated, willing that to be true. "I had a little too much wine. Since I was in no shape to drive, he brought me home." She smacked her forehead with her palm. "I forgot about my car. Can you get away and drive me to the Bar and Grill to pick it up?"

"Sure. I'll be by at lunchtime. Back to last night. I've never seen you drunk."

"I only had three glasses." Suddenly unable to sit still and in need of a second cup of coffee, Cammie carried the receiver over to the counter, where the coffeemaker sat between the toaster and a colorful, but empty, cookie jar. "I'm not even hungover."

But she sure had made a fool of herself. Wrinkling her nose, she refilled her cup, then carried it to the fridge and added milk. Skim, of course. "I just didn't feel I should take the wheel."

"Sounds like the smart thing to do," Jules said. "Does this mean you and Curt are friends again?"

At the door last night Curt had asked the same question, his eyes searching Cammie's. She hadn't known what to say. Despite her best intentions, she liked the man, but that didn't mean she wanted to restart their friendship as if nothing had happened. Still, standing so close to him, *something* had happened. She'd craved his kisses and he'd turned her down.

Even if he *had* kissed her, which since he didn't think of her that way he never would, she wasn't stupid enough to get involved with a man who never wanted to get married and whom she no longer trusted. No matter how attractive he was.

"What it means," she said at last, "is that from now on I'm a one-glass-of-wine woman."

In dire need of a new man in her life. That was the only way to get past this ridiculous lust for Curt Blanco. "And that I'm seriously ready to date again," she added in a bright voice. "So keep your eyes open."

Chapter Four

Bleary-eyed, Cammie yawned as she drove her parents to the Portland airport Saturday morning—a four-plus-hour drive. It was still dark out, and they wouldn't hit the freeway for a good two hours. They had the narrow, winding road to themselves.

"Tired?" her mother asked from the backseat.

"Four a.m. is not my favorite time of the day," she said. Especially since she'd been up late, working on last-minute changes Weston wanted for tonight's dinner party.

"Mine, either," her father said from the passenger seat. Yet he sounded alert and excited. "But our plane leaves for London at ten and they want us there two hours early."

"We probably should have ordered a shuttle and stayed at a motel near the airport," her mother commented from the backseat.

"A shuttle all this way?" Cammie shook her head. "That'd cost way too much. Besides, I won't see you for a full month, so I want to spend this time with you." She yawned again, earning her an insightful look from her father.

"You were up late working on Kelly and Rick's engagement party, weren't you?" he asked.

"I wish we could come," her mother said.

Cammie glanced at her in the rearview mirror. "Don't worry, I'll give you a full report via e-mail."

"We'd appreciate that." Her mother leaned forward, clasping her hands on Cammie's headrest. "I do hope Weston understands."

Her father turned toward her mother. "The expensive bouquet we sent for tonight and our generous wedding gift should ease any ruffled feathers."

Curt had said the same thing. But Cammie didn't want to think about him. Her parents had paid two years' worth of premiums on generous life-insurance policies for Kelly and Rick. "What you gave Kelly and Rick is both wonderful and unique."

"Well, Weston *is* one of our most important clients," her mother said. "And we don't want that to change. Even if he is abrasive and unpleasant. That's his nature. Over the years your dad and I have learned to work around that." She squeezed Cammie's shoulder. "I hope you can, too."

"Of course I can," Cammie said, flashing a reassuring smile in the rearview mirror. For her parents' and Kelly's sakes, she'd do anything to keep Weston happy. "Don't worry about me."

"What about Curt?" her father asked. "Do you think you can work with him?"

As close as Cammie was to her parents, she wasn't about to tell them about her strong physical attraction to Curt, or that she'd thrown herself at him the other night. Some things were private. "I'm a professional. I'll manage," she said, forcing a casual tone.

Her father stroked his chin thoughtfully. "You two made a good team, you handling the events and him taking the pictures. I always did like him, and I'm glad to see you working together again."

"Edwin!" her mother scolded. "Have you forgotten? Curt introduced Cammie to Todd."

"I never held that against him. Wasn't his fault Todd turned out to be a bastard."

Cammie waited for her mother's gasp—she disliked swearing. But she was silent, which proved how deeply she detested Todd. Her parents counted her lucky for finding out about him before the wedding.

"I agree with Dad," Cammie said. "Curt didn't know what Todd was really like."

If her statement surprised them—after all, she'd spent eleven-plus months blaming him—they didn't let on.

For a few moments everyone went silent, all lost in their own thoughts.

"You'll be able to handle a wedding at the Oceanside?" her mother asked at last, sounding worried.

As Cammie opened her mouth to answer, the sound of her father's exasperated breath filled the car. "She wouldn't do it if she wasn't ready."

"I know that, Edwin. I just don't like the idea of our daughter reliving that devastating time. It's only been a year."

"Hello, I'm here so don't talk about me as if I weren't," Cammie reminded them. "Don't worry, I've moved past that whole mess." She hoped.

"That's reassuring to know. Your father and I so want you to meet the right person and fall in love."

"Leave her alone, Peg."

Cammie took her parents' squabbling in stride. They'd lived together thirty-five years and sometimes disagreed. Who wouldn't? No two people could agree on everything. Underneath the petty arguments, they loved each other a great deal.

Taking her gaze from the road a moment, she shot her father a grateful, fond look. "That's okay, Dad. I'm ready to date again and find my soul mate. I want what you and Mom have." She grinned. "Bickering and all."

Her parents chimed in with sheepish chuckles.

"I heard through the grapevine that you and Curt are on the same volleyball team," her mother said, sounding mildly hurt.

"Did I forget to tell you?" Cammie feigned confusion. "Sorry about that. I didn't think it was important."

"Curt and you on the same volleyball team," her father mused. "Huh." Several seconds of silence ticked by before he spoke again. "That guy you're looking for? Keep your eyes open. He's out there."

"And keep us posted," her mother added. "We'll be checking our e-mail every few days, and we'll call when we can."

"Great. Anything you want me to do while you're gone? Besides water the lawn and the houseplants."

"That's it," her mother said. "Just please remind Kelly and Weston how very sorry we are about missing all the festivities. If only she'd scheduled the wedding one week later…"

For the rest of the trip, which included a stop for gas and a bathroom break, they made small talk. At the airport at last, Cammie pulled to a stop. Since she couldn't go to the gate with her parents and she needed to hurry back and attend to last-minute details for tonight's party, she didn't park.

She did get out to stretch her legs and help with the luggage. When the suitcases were safely out of the trunk and piled onto a baggage cart, she hugged her mother, who at fifty-five was still trim and young looking. "Have a wonderful time."

Her mother's hug was warm and hard. "I'll miss you, honey."

"It's only four weeks," her father said. He embraced Cammie, then kissed her forehead. "You keep your eyes open for that special fella."

"Maybe she'll find him while we're gone," her mother added, her eyes twinkling.

Cammie fervently hoped so. "Have a wonderful trip. I'll pick you up on the eleventh."

FEELING LIKE A MOTHER HEN, Cammie hovered anxiously on the kitchen side of a swinging door that led to the dining room of Weston Atwood's spacious home. From here she could spy unobserved through the maid's window on the door.

The hors d'oeuvres and cocktails had been served and enjoyed. Now everyone was at the table, seated according to the chart prepared by her and revised twice by Weston. In true it's-my-party form, he presided over his long dining-room table and the four circular tables arranged in the foyer as well. His voice dominated at this first party in honor of Kelly and Rick's engagement. Most of tonight's guests were locals—friends and family. Cammie knew them all and had planned events for several.

Six tuxedo-clad men and women from the catering company she'd hired served and attended to the forty-eight guests' every whim with delicacies from the menu she had planned and Weston had, naturally, amended.

Keeping a close eye on the details, answering questions and solving unanticipated problems was a stressful, exhausting part of her job, and only five hours' sleep last night and nearly nine hours on the road this morning didn't help. But right now Cammie was too keyed up to feel tired. Her payoff was the obvious enjoyment Weston, Kelly, Rick and their guests shared tonight.

The party had begun two hours earlier. As the crowd had whetted their appetites with cocktails and conversation, Curt had worked unobtrusively, snapping candid shots of the happy occasion. Now he moved among the five tables, capturing joyous moments. The guests didn't seem to notice, which was how Curt liked to work. Cammie noticed, though. He would have to wear that crisp, blue dress shirt; those gray slacks; and the silver-and-navy striped tie.

Moving around the main table, he paused and aimed his Leica at Kelly and Rick, heads bent as they conversed in low, intimate voices. Cammie smiled at the radiant couple before her attention again shifted to Curt.

Standing behind the kitchen door, she could only see him from the back, but oh, what a back it was. As he focused the camera, his broad shoulders strained the fabric of his shirt. He always had been buff, but until the past week she'd never truly noticed how long his back was. Or his small, tight rear end…

Giving herself a mental shake, she frowned. She hadn't had one drop of wine since Thursday, yet here she was, drooling as if she'd drunk a bottle. That would stop this instant. Since they were working together, she would be civil. Professional, as she'd told her parents. She really did need a distraction, some nice, handsome, trustworthy male. Maybe one of tonight's guests… Not that she meant to do anything tonight, of course. But looking couldn't hurt.

She surveyed the main table and each of the others. Most of the men were paired up with wives or girlfriends. Her gaze homed in on sandy-haired Dwight Swanson, the only man without a partner. A CPA, Dwight handled the taxes for all the Atwood holdings. Cammie wasn't attracted to him—he was several years older than she—but he *was* single with an excellent job and a sterling reputation. Unfortunately, he still lived with his mother. She wrinkled her nose and decided to search elsewhere. On Tuesday, at volleyball.

Servers nudged past her to deliver salads. Cammie followed the last server out and took her place visibly but silently at the door, where she could watch them serve. There was plenty to keep her mind off Curt, yet as diners finished their salads and the servers collected empty plates, her attention returned to him.

As if he felt her staring, he glanced her way. Though they were a good thirty feet apart, she saw his eyes warm. Her body began to tingle and hum. Maybe he was attracted to her, too…. The moment the thought entered her mind, his eyes shuttered like a closing camera lens. He gave a pained, solemn nod, and somehow she knew he was remembering the other night.

Inwardly she winced. Outwardly she matched his unhappy expression and returned the terse nod. Weston, who never missed anything and who expected the hired help to smile at all times, narrowed his eyes, first at Cammie and then at Curt. Pretending not to notice, she again followed the last server through the swinging door and into the kitchen.

"That went very well," she said as the chef ladled steaming sherry-mushroom soup into delicate china bowls. "You're all doing super jobs." Everyone looked pleased. "Are you ready to—"

Suddenly Weston barreled into the room, Curt at his heels. Curt made a slashing gesture across his neck, which Weston didn't see.

Everyone else did. Looking nervous, the servers quickly slid the bowls onto their trays and moved toward the door. The chef bowed to his work, stirring sauces and checking steaming pots.

Face mottled, eyes glaring, Weston jerked his thumb toward the empty breakfast room on the other side of the kitchen.

Cammie could think of nothing she'd done to displease him. He demanded pomp and circumstance, and she'd provided it. He wanted abundant, expensive alcohol and high-quality, well-prepared food, and she'd provided those, too.

"What's going on?" she whispered, exchanging a nervous look with Curt.

"Beats me," he replied in a low voice. "I was in the middle of shooting photos when he 'summoned' me."

Weston wheeled on them. "What's 'going on,'" he said, sneering, "is those scowls on your faces. People are watching you two instead of Rick and my Kelly."

Cammie knew why. Everyone here knew about her

canceled wedding and subsequent falling out with Curt. No doubt the guests wondered about them working together tonight. With Weston's red face and nasty expression, they probably were doubly curious. The entire kitchen had gone silent. Cammie was humiliated, and glad her parents weren't here. For their and Kelly's sakes, she bowed her head and let the man vent.

"Your personal feelings are your business, but at my functions you will smile and pretend you're the best of friends, or else," Weston hissed. "Now, say something nice to each other."

He glared expectantly at Curt.

Who looked Cammie over, from her hair to her teal-colored cocktail dress, to her strappy, black patent-leather sandals. "Nice outfit," he said, his eyes bright with appreciation. "And great party."

She felt her cheeks flush with pleasure. "Thanks."

Weston eyed Cammie. "Your turn."

Not about to comment on *his* clothes, she glanced at his camera. "You're working really hard tonight. I know the pictures will be great."

Curt looked gratified. "Thanks for noticing."

Because Weston expected it, she smiled. Curt smiled back.

Weston's jaw unclenched. "That's better."

Without another word, he pivoted away and strode through the kitchen to the dining room, his mean face morphing into the amiable host's before he rejoined his guests.

"That was fun," Curt muttered. "But I meant what I said." His gaze warmed again. "You look hot."

Cammie melted, but refused to let on. "What happened to that grin? You heard the man." She drew a smile in the air, then pointed at Curt's mouth.

He swore, then curled his lips in the worst parody of a happy man she'd ever seen.

The anger glinting in his eyes worried her. Tonight was no time for a scene that could ruin Kelly's evening and risk their jobs. "Remember our agreement," she reminded him.

The ludicrous smile vanished. "I know, I know, do whatever King Atwood commands. I wish there was another paper in town, because working for Weston is a pain in the butt."

"It certainly is." Cammie sighed. "But Kelly's happiness means everything to me. And you need this job...."

Weston's bellowing laugh filled the air. "It's showtime." Cammie glued a smile on her face.

Fake grin back in place, Curt gestured toward the dining room. "After you."

"GET A LOAD OF YOUR BROTHER," Eric said to Curt as they headed into the gym on Tuesday night.

Curt glanced across the wood floor at Steven, who had begged off the before-volleyball dinner at Kit and Eric's to eat with Jules. Now his arm was around her, which was no big deal. But that lovesick smile was painful. Curt shook his head. "Never thought I'd see him so whipped. Lucky dog must be getting some good sex."

Eric shook his head. "I don't think so."

Since Blanco men didn't kiss and tell, he didn't really know. Curt frowned. "What makes you say that?"

"If they were sleeping together, would he be looking at her like he wanted to gobble her up?"

"Maybe," Curt said. "If the sex was really great."

"I think he's holding back."

"That doesn't sound like Steven. Why would he do that?"

"Because he really likes Jules. I was like that with Kit," Eric explained. "I knew she was the One, and waiting a while made the event all the more meaningful."

"Interesting." Curt tried to understand but came up empty. "Makes no sense to me."

"You haven't fallen in love yet."

"And I never will. Too many fine women out there."

"Steven used to say the same thing, and we know Jules likes variety." Eric smirked at the besotted couple. "Now look at them."

Curt did. "Jules looks like she wants to gobble Steven up, too," he said. "Could be, they're just horny."

"Then what's stopping them from doing the nasty?"

Eric had a good point. Curt eyed him. "So you think this is serious?"

His brother shrugged. "Time will tell."

Curt spotted Cammie as she, Marcy and several other attractive females strolled from the girls' locker room. "Here come some of those fine women now."

Lots of legs and breasts to check out and lust over. But his wayward attention fixed on Cammie. Tonight she wore lemon-yellow shorts and a matching T-shirt. Not as sexy as her clingy cocktail dress Saturday night, but hot all the same.

Following Curt's gaze, Eric glanced at Cammie, who hadn't noticed either of them. Then, brows raised, he eyed Curt. "How'd things go at that party Saturday night?"

"Weston was his usual domineering self, but I took some great photos."

"I meant between you and Cammie."

"Not great," Curt replied. Before Weston had threatened them, she'd mostly glared at Curt. After that her fixed smile had never made it to her eyes. Which told him what he already knew—she could barely stand him. That kiss she'd begged for after volleyball last week? Too much wine and nothing more. "She still doesn't trust me, but I'm working on that."

"That must be why she isn't smiling," Eric said. "I better head over to my team. See you after practice. Unless you're going to the Bar and Grill again."

No way did Curt want to risk sitting across the table from Cammie, where he could watch her face and that long neck. He shook his head. "Not tonight."

The women in Cammie's group split up to join their respective teams. Looking less than thrilled to see him, Cammie sauntered over, Marcy at her side.

Curt thanked God he hadn't given in to temptation and kissed her the other night. If he had, she'd likely be snarling at him.

"Hi," Marcy said. For once she didn't bat her lashes or stick out her chest.

Curt nodded. "Hey."

"Have you seen Billy?"

"In the men's locker room." Unlike the Blanco men, Billy liked to share his exploits. He'd crowed plenty about his weekend in bed with Marcy, but Curt wasn't about to say so. "He should be out soon."

"There he is." Giving her head a provocative shake, Marcy sashayed toward Billy. Leaving Curt alone with Cammie.

"Here we are again," he said, forming his lips into a big, fake smile.

Cammie did the same.

"If Weston could see us now," he quipped.

To his relief, she laughed. "After his little talk, I think he was satisfied with our behavior."

"He didn't talk, he threatened." Curt was still ticked about that.

"I know." The last traces of laughter faded from her face. "Thanks for keeping your cool."

"I gave you my word, didn't I?" Mentally Curt patted himself on the back for gaining brownie points. "You can count on me."

Instead of agreeing that, yes, indeed, she could trust him, she offered a skeptical look. Disappointing, but not unexpected.

At least they were talking. Not in the chummy, warm way they used to, but better than cold silence.

Definite progress, and there were still almost four weeks before the wedding. Time was on Curt's side, and he knew that, sooner or later, he would earn back her trust and regain her friendship.

"You're in charge of that eighth-grade graduation dance Friday night at Town Hall, right?" he asked.

Thanks to a basketball game in the gym that night and an agreement with the city, the party would be at Town Hall, where space was available and rent was cheap.

Cammie nodded. "Are you the photographer?"

"Who else?" As the photographer for the *Cranberry News Weekly*, he always photographed class parties, which were newsworthy events in a town the size of Cranberry. He also had a standing contract with the school to handle class photos, student ID cards and any yearbook pictures not covered by the yearbook staff. "Looks as if we're working together on that, too," he said.

She didn't appear to have heard, her attention on Pete Gillespie, a quarterback-size fireman Steven's age. As he sauntered toward his teammates across the gym, her gaze turned speculative. "What do you know about Pete?"

"Why?" he asked, barely managing to keep the edge from his voice.

"I think he's cute."

Not something Curt wanted to know. He frowned. "And you're telling me this because…?"

"Maybe I'm interested in him."

"Pete's almost as wild as Billy." Curt leveled a look at her to make sure she got the message. "He's not your type."

"Oh." A deflated sigh slipped from her lips.

"You'll find the right man," Curt said, as a true friend would.

But the thought of Cammie with any guy, even a decent one, didn't sit well with him. Which made no sense at all. She deserved happiness, and for her that meant a ring and forever.

Billy and Marcy strolled toward them, arms around each other's waists, wearing matching looks of sexual satisfaction and the expectation of more to come. Curt envied them that.

Mike Anderson, their team captain, and the rest of their teammates joined them. They moved as a group to the volleyball net set up for their practice.

As they crossed the gym, Curt scoped out several of the women. None of them interested him. He glanced at Cammie and his body stirred. His bad luck that the only female who did was the one he'd never pursue. Even if he did hit on her, and he wasn't about to go there, Cammie would reject him. And rightly so.

He wanted her friendship. Period. No matter what his body told him.

Chapter Five

Curt, his brothers and Kit often shared Sunday dinner with his father and, when time allowed, visited him during the week. It'd been a few weeks since Curt had dropped by, so busy as he was, Friday he made a mid-morning stop at the bungalow on the edge of town. On his way up the stone path to the front door, he glanced around. Earlier it had rained but now the sun was bright and warm, which was great for the plants and rough on the people who mowed the lawns. Only a week ago Curt's brothers had come to take care of the yard work, yet before long the grass would need cutting and edging again. This was a big yard. No flowers or vegetable garden, but even so, taking care of it took a few hours. He made a mental note to talk to his brothers and set up a Sunday in the near future.

Wiping his feet on the faded jute mat, he knocked on the weathered door, which wasn't locked. "It's me, Pop."

"Come on in."

Curt walked into the living room. The green shag carpeting he'd grown up with had seen better days, but thanks to the cleaning lady they'd hired, it was vacuumed.

His father waved from his favorite plaid-covered armchair that faced the TV, which was turned to one of the morning talk shows.

He still had all his hair, gray now at the temples, and the Blanco good looks. But since the accident almost seven months earlier he'd aged a decade, no doubt from the pain that always was with him. And getting worse, according to Kit, who had come by a few days earlier.

"How's it going?" he asked, dropping onto the nearby sofa, its faded, striped slipcover a leftover of long-gone wife number four.

"Just ducky." Eyes on the remote, his pop pressed the mute button. "How're you?"

He knew about Curt's falling out with Cammie, but not that they were working together again. Curt saw no sense in mentioning that until he had something to say— until they were friends again. So he shrugged. "Not bad."

"What brings you out here on a workday?"

"It's been too long." True enough, but the real reason Curt was here was to get his father to seek help for his increasing pain. A stubborn cuss, he wouldn't do it unless Curt or his brothers pushed him. He noted the grim lines around his pop's mouth, and frowned. "When is your next appointment with Dr. Scheyer?"

"A few weeks from now."

"You ought to see him now and tell him your pain is worse."

"Did Kit blab?" Curt's father rolled his eyes. "I knew I shouldn't have told her."

"I'm glad you did. Why don't you call him, Pop?"

"What for? He'll just prescribe more physical therapy and pain meds." His pop snorted. "Fat lot of good that does me."

"There must be something else he can do," Curt said. "You want me to call and ask about alternatives?"

"Hell, no." A proud, independent man, Burton Blanco shook his head. "I'll do that myself, if that'll get you boys and Kit off my back. But even if he comes up with something new, we both know there's no insurance to pay for it."

Curt felt crappy about that. They all did. He wished he could take away his father's pain for good, but all he could do was make sure he got good medical care. "Look," he said. "What's important is that you get rid of the pain. Don't worry about the money. Steven, Eric and I will pay the bills, just like we've been doing."

"You already do too much. Hell, you can barely keep up with the current medical bills." His father shook his head and made a face, as if he smelled rotting food. "Maybe if you had the money in the bank, but you don't." He tightened his mouth. "I'm not about to put you three deeper into the poorhouse. One bankruptcy in the family is more than enough."

Curt opened his mouth to argue but a rude gesture from his father cut him off. "You must have too much time on your hands. Know what you need? A woman to take your mind off me. How long since you've been laid, anyway?"

"Pop!" Curt felt his face heat. "That's none of your business."

"Yeah but you forgot about me for a minute there, didn't you?"

His father chuckled, stopping mid-laugh to wince

with pain. He noted Curt's distressed expression and scowled. "Get outta here now, and go earn your living. And find yourself a lady."

MINUTES BEFORE the eighth-grade party was due to start, Cammie glanced around the large Town Hall meeting room she'd secured for tonight. The decorations for the Anchors Aweigh! themed evening had transformed the ordinary space into an ocean fantasy complete with revolving mirror ball, fishnets draped and hanging from the ceiling, plastic sea creatures, a sunken ship and a treasure chest full of gold foil-wrapped chocolate coins.

Corny, but the class had voted on this theme and had raised the money to fund it, and Cammie aimed to please.

The food table was laden with finger foods and an assortment of pop, and decorated with more netting and several large mermaids, their breasts tastefully covered by their long hair.

In the far corner, three parents, two teachers and Chet Avery, the principal, were huddled together, reviewing their roles as chaperones. On stage, a local DJ Cammie had hired, a balding, friendly man—not the popular Steven Blanco, as he was working another party—checked the sound system and the mike.

Everything was set for a great evening—for the kids, anyway. It would be busy and hectic for Cammie. And with Curt soon to show up, nerve-racking. Not that she begrudged him the job. He needed the money for his father's medical expenses, and he *was* the best. But working with him on the wedding, playing volleyball with him and now this? She didn't need the distraction.

Suddenly an authoritative knock sounded at the

locked double doors that opened into the hallway. That was probably him now. Ignoring her wayward heart, which lifted in expectation, Cammie unlocked one door, opened it a fraction and peeked through. Anxious voices of adolescents eager to come inside filled the air. When she saw Curt, she opened the door. Armed with his camera, bulging shoulder bag and a pull cart containing a screen, tripod and special lighting, he made his way inside. Cammie shut the door behind him and re-locked it, cutting off the adolescent voices.

"The entire class is out there, waiting to get in," he said.

"So I heard."

As always he looked fit and handsome, though thanks to the blustery May weather, his hair was wind-blown. A thick swatch hung rakishly over his forehead, making him look like a carefree playboy. He wasn't rich enough to qualify, but certainly shared the play-around-and-don't-get-serious attitude.

Cammie knew that. She knew Curt wasn't for her, yet her stomach felt fluttery and her nerves went on alert.

Her reaction stymied her. Darn it, after years of friendship and nothing more, after they'd parted ways, why was she attracted to him *now?*

"You'd think those kids hadn't seen each other in school a few hours ago." He set down his load, pulled a red tie from the pocket of his tan sport coat and looped it under his collar.

Cammie shrugged. "Hormones, I guess."

"You said it, and they'll all be in this room." His gaze traveled the large space. "I hardly recognize this place. Nice decor."

"Thanks."

"It's gonna be an interesting evening," he said, looking as if he'd rather be someplace else.

"Take heart. By ten o'clock it'll all be over. Anybody can survive two and a half hours."

His mouth quirked. "I hope you're right."

"Me, too. Where do you want to set up?"

"That sunken boat in the corner will make a nice backdrop for photos."

"Perfect," she said, making a mental note to steer clear of the area. If she avoided Curt and kept him out of her line of sight, maybe she wouldn't think about him so much. "Do you need help carrying your stuff?"

"No, thanks." He hefted his things.

Cammie watched him walk away, his shoulders bunching under the awkward load of equipment. Even loaded down, he was gorgeous. A sigh of admiration slipped from her lips. If only she could find a man to take her mind off Curt...

Jules was supposed to be on the lookout for interesting prospects, but lately she was no help. She was so wrapped up in Steven, she barely had time for Cammie. Finding time together was no easy task, so they were having breakfast at Rosy's tomorrow, just the two of them. Nothing leisurely, since Cammie and Kelly were driving to Portland for a fitting, but better than nothing.

Chet Avery glanced at the clock—exactly seven-thirty—and nodded at Cammie to unlock the doors. Like a gust of wind, forty-three eighth graders dressed in party clothes gushed en masse into the room. Within seconds they were clumped into groups segregated by gender and other factors known only to them, their nervousness as palpable as their artificial laughter. Tonight was a dance, but since at fourteen these kids weren't old enough to date, the event was more like an awkward social gathering of boys versus girls.

The DJ introduced himself and kicked off the evening with a hip-hop song. Aside from nervous glances at the chaperones standing on the perimeter, no one moved for several minutes. Then a group of giggling girls with long legs and skinny torsos moved onto the floor and started dancing.

For the next two hours Cammie was busy attending to the food, games and contests—details that made the evening run smoothly. Despite that, and despite the fact that she kept her back to Curt, she was keenly aware of him.

More than once she caught herself glancing his way, first where he set up the screen and tripod to snap individual photos of kids in their good clothes, and later, as he moved around the room taking candid shots for the *Cranberry News*.

Near the end of the evening he moved to her side. "Brings back memories, doesn't it?" he asked as he aimed the camera at various dancing couples, the girls inevitably taller and more mature than their partners.

They'd both attended a similar graduation dance in eighth grade. Cammie shook her head. "Were we as gawky and high-strung as these kids?"

"I was," Curt said. Photography forgotten for the moment, he glanced at her. "Remember how a bunch of us sneaked into the town council chambers to play spin the bottle?"

For Cammie, the long-ago event was a hazy memory, but a few details floated back. "That was the first time you and I actually met. As I recall, we were the first couple to step into the coat closet."

Curt nodded. "You wore a short, white dress and your first pair of heels—I heard you tell somebody that—and your hair was long and wavy. You tucked one side behind one ear with a gardenia."

Cammie's jaw dropped. "You remember all *that?*"

"I remember every detail of that half hour. When you spun that empty Coke bottle and it stopped facing me, I couldn't believe my luck. I was so nervous, I knocked a bunch of hangers down. Made quite a noise."

Smiling at the memory, Cammie nodded. "I remember that. We were scared somebody would hear and we'd get caught."

"I didn't care," Curt said. "Kissing you was worth the risk."

Cammie hadn't known that. "Why?" she asked, angling her head.

"You were the first girl I ever kissed, and one of the coolest girls in eighth grade. No fear of getting caught was going to stop me."

"I was your first kiss?" Surprised at this news flash, she widened her eyes. "All the years I've known you and you're just now telling me this?"

"I didn't think it mattered."

"Well, it did. Was I any good?"

"You were amazing."

His chocolate eyes, dark and very warm, sought hers. Awareness shivered up her spine.

"But I sucked," he said in a dry tone. "I've had a lot of practice since then, though. I'm better at it now."

"So they say."

"Yeah?" He smiled devilishly, charming her. "What've you heard?"

She hadn't exactly heard firsthand, but once at a bridal shower she'd hosted, a vocal group of slightly drunk women had gathered in the kitchen and shared stories of their best lovers. Stuff that should be private. Blushing furiously, Cammie had shamelessly eavesdropped while she'd gathered her things. Curt's name had been mentioned, along with the adjectives *generous* and *passionate*.

Oh, to experience some of that passion for herself… Her body thrummed, and for one instant she thought about pulling him back into that closet in the other room to find out for herself. But that would never happen. Cammie shook her head. "If I told you, you'd get even cockier than you already are. One thing I remember about our party was that Tim Martin and Bobby Rush threw up outside the boy's bathroom. Luckily, that hasn't happened tonight."

"I don't remember that at all," Curt said. "I do recall that by Monday, you and Marcus Vaneer were going steady. That about killed me."

Cammie scoffed. "I doubt that."

"It's true," he said. "I thought I was in love with you, and when you got together with Marcus right after our kiss, you broke my heart."

This was news to Cammie. Wondering whether Curt was joking, she waited for a teasing grin. His somber expression and steady gaze never wavered, and she knew he hadn't lied. She bit her lip. "You never told me."

"You were part of the cool crowd, and I wasn't. I was afraid you'd reject me, and I couldn't bear the humiliation. When we got older…" He shrugged, then squinted through his camera lens to snap a picture. "By then we were good friends, and my crush was old news." He clicked the shutter again, his expression hidden behind the camera. "Would it have mattered if I told you?"

Cammie wished she could see his face. "I honestly don't know," she said. "But I'm sorry if I hurt you."

When he finally glanced at her, his expression was unreadable. "It was a long time ago. You're forgiven—if you agree to be friends."

He looked so serious. Cammie wanted to see his smile. Against her better judgment she wanted his friendship, too. She sighed. "All right, I'll try the friendship thing, on a trial basis." Wait till Jules hears about this. "Just please, don't ever fix me up again."

As she'd hoped, his expression lightened. "Scout's honor," he said, giving the Boy Scout salute.

"You know," she said, again thinking back to eighth grade, "Marcus told me he loved me, and I believed him. A few weeks later he cheated on me with Samantha Tiggles, and we broke up. He was fifteen and I was barely fourteen, but still." She wrinkled her nose. "Even back then I chose the untrustworthy guy." Half-teasing, half-serious, she shook her head. "I wonder why I seem to gravitate toward that kind of man?"

"Because most of us are rats," Curt said. "But I'm your friend, and as a friend, you can trust me."

With his eyes big and soulful, he definitely looked trustworthy. Wise or not, Cammie decided to go with that. On a trial basis.

The DJ moved to the mike. "It's almost ten o'clock, people, and this is the last set," he announced, playing a fast-paced oldies song. "So mix it up!"

"Ten o'clock? Feels like midnight to me," Curt quipped. "You were right, we survived."

"Somehow." Cammie was exhausted, both from dealing with adolescents and from battling her attraction to Curt.

"I'll pack up my stuff and stow it in the CR-V, then come back to give you a hand with the cleanup."

"You don't have to do that," she said. "Six of the kids here tonight have volunteered to help."

"You're tired, aren't you? One more person will make it go all the faster. Come on, Cam," he said, using his old nickname for her.

She liked when he called her that. What she didn't like was the warm, happy feeling in her heart. Silently and sternly she reminded herself that Curt wasn't the man she wanted. Except as a friend. Tentatively. "Okay," she said. "I'm glad for the extra help."

Curt flashed an irresistible grin. "Back in a few, buddy."

CURT WAS TIRED, AND CLEANING up after a bunch of kids was at the bottom of his wish list. But with him and Cammie getting along so well, he wasn't about to leave. The half-dozen energetic eighth graders helping made the job a quick one, and they finished in no time.

The kids left. Alone with Cammie, he fell into step beside her as she headed for the council chambers, the building eerily silent. Moments later she grabbed her purse, yellow leather jacket and a dolly from the closet— the very place where they'd kissed.

"Here we are, at the scene of the crime," he said.

Not wanting her to realize how long he'd carried a torch for her, through high school and into college, he'd glossed over his feelings. Thank God he was over all that. Now he wanted only friendship.

Yet a crazy idea grabbed him, to pull her into the closet and kiss her, to see what that felt like. He squelched the urge, fast. She was beginning to trust him again, and he didn't want to jeopardize that.

"Not a very romantic place for a person's first kiss," Cammie commented.

"As I said earlier, I'd have kissed you anyplace."

This time she rolled her eyes. "Enough already! Speaking of kissing, what do you know about Steven and Jules?"

"Not much except he's spending an awful lot of time with her." Curt eyed her. "Why, what do you know?"

She shrugged. "About the same. I'll be heading to Portland with Kelly tomorrow to meet with her dress-maker, but first Jules and I are having breakfast. Maybe she'll fill me in then."

"Then would you please fill *me* in?" Curt asked. "Because Steven isn't talking."

"Unless she asks me not to." The closet door closed with a soft click.

"I'll help carry stuff to your car," he said, taking hold of the dolly.

"I'll let you."

He knew the drill. They piled the dolly with boxes of stuff Cammie either owned or had rented. He made two trips, leaving boxes on the curb by her car. With the third load, one box remained. Cammie grabbed it. Curt wheeled the dolly forward, and they headed through the doors and down the empty hall.

They walked in companionable silence, something

they hadn't done in nearly a year. Most women couldn't handle silence more than a few seconds, but Cammie never had minded long stretches of it. That was one of the things Curt liked about her.

Their cars, the only vehicles in the parking lot, sat side by side near the door. Tall parking lights illuminated the lot, and the air smelled of the nearby sea. Curt squinted at the sky, unable to see much. It had been cloudy when he'd arrived and likely still was. Typical May weather, including the brisk wind.

A gust whisked Cammie's hair off her face and flattened her short, flouncy skirt against her luscious, round behind. Curt's blood stirred.

"Whew!" she shrieked, laughing. She cupped her hands over her head. She hated her naturally curly hair, and spent time every morning straightening it with a gizmo that removed the curl.

His hair slapped his forehead and his slacks whipped the back of his legs, and he, too, laughed. Cammie beamed at him, and suddenly he felt as if he were back in eighth grade, captivated by the sparkle in her eyes and the delight on her face. But he was thirty-one now, no dumb kid. And *not* attracted to her.

Sobering, he bowed into the wind and pushed the dolly toward the green minivan she used for her business.

She unlocked the back. Together they loaded boxes, both from the curb and the dolly, inside. When they finished, she brushed her hands together, closed the back gate and turned to him.

"Thanks for the help," she said, smoothing her fingers through her hair. A useless activity, since the wind messed it right back up again.

"My pleasure." Hardly aware of what he was doing, he leaned toward her. "I had fun with you, Cammie, and I'm glad we're friends again."

She shot him a guarded look.

"Probationary friends," he amended, watching her expression to see how she liked that.

A little nod said she did. "I had a good time, too."

Curt bent down to kiss her cheek, the way he used to.

At the same time Cammie turned her head. Abruptly their lips were mere inches apart. He smelled her lily-of-the-valley perfume. He felt the tantalizing warmth from her peaches-and-cream skin. Her eyelids lowered a fraction, her chin tipped up, and her perfect lips went into kiss formation. The temptation was too great to fight.

He had to kiss her. One chaste peck—he wanted to keep her trust—and he'd back off. He brushed his mouth over hers in a quick, friendly good-night.

Trouble was, her lips were soft and warm, and her breath smelled sweet, like the peppermints she kept in her purse. Her eyes were dark and unfocused, yet also intent with feeling, and he couldn't seem to pull away.

Then her eyelids drifted shut and her arms looped around his neck. Her hips settled tightly against his and her soft breasts pressed his chest.

The same as the other night, when she'd drunk too much wine. Only this time she was as sober as he was.

And he was lost.

CAMMIE KNEW SHE SHOULDN'T KISS Curt this way, but the feel of his lips intoxicated her. She hadn't been kissed like this—she hadn't been kissed at all—since she'd broken off with Todd, and her starved body pulsed to life.

Curt's skilled lips teased and coaxed her to deeper, openmouthed kisses. Without reservation or hesitation she matched his fervor, tangling her tongue with his.

A throaty sound purled from his chest. He was aroused. She felt the hard proof against her lower belly. So was she. Already the place between her legs was damp and throbbing.

That scared her. Curt wasn't the man for her. This was wrong!

He seemed to have the same idea, for they jerked apart at the same moment.

Cammie tugged down her magenta sweater, which had somehow gotten bunched around her waist. She couldn't help but glance at the erection straining Curt's trousers.

Following her gaze, he made a sound of disapproval. "I didn't mean for this to happen," he said. "Friends don't kiss like that."

She thought he might apologize, but he didn't seem sorry. Cammie wasn't either. Her body was tingling and yearning. This bothered her. She didn't want to feel hunger for Curt, who was supposed to be her friend. Provisionally, they'd agreed.

"You are right about one thing," she said, striving to add humor to the situation. "You're a much better kisser than you were in eighth grade."

He didn't crack a smile. "Under any other circumstance, I'd be happy to hear that." He cast her a worried look. "Are we okay? Did I screw things up?"

Oh, yes. Cammie shook her head. "Just don't kiss me that way ever again."

Looking relieved, he released a breath. "That's a deal."

Chapter Six

Sharing Saturday breakfast with Jules was an occasional event Cammie savored. Unfortunately, tourist season had started with a bang, and Rosy's was packed. Three harried waitresses, Rosy included, bustled from table to table, with barely time for smiles of welcome. Cammie's favorite booth in the front window was taken, with nothing available except a table for four in the back corner.

Jules wanted to watch the people, so Cammie faced the wall and a framed map of Cranberry. She liked to watch people, too, but today she didn't care where she sat or what her view was, as long as she and Jules caught each other up on their lives.

The instant they sat down, Rosy filled their mugs with steaming coffee. "Good to see you girls this morning," she said, taking time for them despite the crowd. "How did the eighth-grade dance go?"

Cammie smiled. "Fine."

"Nothing out of the ordinary?" Rosy prodded. "No fights, kids caught kissing or drinking to share with my customers?"

"Sorry, none that I know of." *Except that Curt kissed*

me and I can't stop thinking about that or wanting more. Those kisses had been a mistake no one would ever know about, and Cammie would not think about them or Curt again. "This year's group was exceptionally well behaved."

"What a letdown." Rosy's disappointment was almost comical. She whipped her order pad from the pocket of her bubble-gum-pink uniform. "You know what you want, or should I come back? Aside from a pair of cranberry juices." As a way to support the local employee-owned cranberry factory, every food establishment and bed-and-breakfast served the juice with breakfast.

"I'm ready," Jules said. "I'll have the ham-and-cheese omelet and a cranberry muffin. And keep the coffee coming."

Rosy scribbled the order, then glanced at Cammie. "For you?"

"Oatmeal with nonfat milk."

Jules made a *phht* sound and waved her hand dismissively. "That's what you always order."

"So what?" Cammie stiffened. "I'm watching my weight."

"What for? You look fine."

"These days, men like their women thin," Rosy said, shooting Cammie a knowing smile. "I'm real glad you've decided to date again."

Naturally she would know that. Most likely everyone in town did. "That and my outfit for Kelly's wedding. After breakfast, she and I are driving to Portland to meet with her dressmaker, and I want to look my best." Not bloated from a big breakfast. "We're planning to spend the night and come back Sunday afternoon."

Rosy nodded her approval. "Sounds fun." She slid the order pad into her pocket.

"Back to dating," Cammie said. "If you know of any eligible men…"

"I'll keep my eyes and ears open." Rosy winked.

As she bustled off, Jules frowned. "You know better than to tell nosy Rosy anything. What's gotten into you?"

"Why not tell her? I'm anxious to meet someone, and she knows everybody. Who knows, she might come up with Mr. Right." A man to take her mind off Curt.

"Nobody from the volleyball league interests you?"

Curt, Cammie thought before she could stop herself. She shook her head. "Not so far." She couldn't stifle a yawn.

Jules scrutinized her. "No offense, but you look tired."

Cammie *was* tired. Those steamy kisses with Curt last night had filled her with a strange restlessness, and she'd had a tough time falling asleep. The same edginess was with her still, making her long for things she had no business wanting, not with Curt. She wasn't sure what to say, so she turned the topic to Jules.

"No more tired than you," she said, nodding at the circles under Jules's eyes. Her mouth twitched. "You and Steven must be getting along *very* well."

She expected a satisfied grin, not a heartfelt sigh. "Steven won't make love with me," Jules lamented. "He says we have something special and he wants to wait."

"Wow." Envy bit with a pang, and Cammie, too, sighed. Would she ever meet a man as wonderful as that? "I can't imagine a man caring that much about me. You two *do* have something special."

"Tell that to my body." Resting her cheek on her

palm, Jules gave her head a dismal shake. "I'm losin' it, Cammie. If something doesn't change, and soon, I swear, I'll explode. I've seriously considered dropping Steven and moving on. Except I don't want to. I think I'm falling for him."

Cammie couldn't stem a cynical smile. "Where have I heard that before?"

"This time, I mean it. My heart tells me Steven is the one, the man I'll be spending the rest of my life with." A dreamy, faraway look clouded her eyes before she frowned. "If I don't die of frustration first."

"The rest of your life?" Cammie gaped in surprise at her friend. "In all the years I've known you, I never heard you say that."

"I never felt like this."

"If you and Steven spend the rest of your lives together, there'll be plenty of time for sex. Can't you relax and let nature take its course?"

"I'm a modern woman, Cammie. I don't want to wait. Hmm." Jules cast a pensive look into space. "We're supposed to see a movie tonight. Maybe when he picks me up I'll open the door in my black see-through teddy, and we'll make our own private movie." The idea seemed to brighten her spirits, and she straightened her shoulders. "But enough about my problems. What's *your* reason for not sleeping?"

At that very moment Rosy appeared with breakfast. While waiting for her to leave, Cammie debated exactly what to tell Jules. She didn't really want to share the details of what had happened last night, but Jules *was* her best friend. She needed advice.

She glanced at Rosy, who was taking a long time to

refill their coffee cups. "May I help you with something, Rosy?"

The waitress shrugged. "I'm curious, too, as to why you didn't sleep well last night."

Stifling the urge to roll her eyes, Cammie opened two packets of artificial sweetener and emptied them on the oatmeal. "I appreciate your interest, but what I have to say is for Jules's ears only."

The unflappable Rosy didn't seem the least bit offended. "Sure, hon. But if you need sleep remedies, the second-best way after having a man to cozy up with is a hot toddy or two." Chuckling, she bustled off.

"If I know Rosy, she'll be telling every single man in town about your sleep troubles," Jules said. She stabbed a mouthful of omelet, popped it into her mouth and murmured her pleasure. Swallowing, she fixed Cammie with an eagle-eyed stare. "Well? What kept you awake last night?" She dropped her attention to her plate to stab another forkful.

"Not what" Cammie said as she drenched her oatmeal with skim milk. "Who"

Eyes wide, Jules set down her fork. "Don't tell me you had sex last night. It's about time, but jeez Louise, how I envy you."

"Well, stop it, because I didn't," Cammie said.

"Who is this mystery guy—at least I assume it's some male—disturbing your sleep?"

Cammie leaned toward her. "Promise you won't repeat even a hint of what I'm about to tell you?"

Nodding, Jules pretended to lock her mouth. "You have my word." She leaned forward and lowered her voice. "Go on."

"You know the kids last night wanted photos. Well, Curt—"

"Blanco?" Jules interrupted so loudly, Cammie was sure Rosy heard clear across the room.

"Keep it down," she warned, pressing her finger to her lips.

"Sorry," Jules said in a softer voice. "Go on."

"We made up last night, and now we're supposed to be friends again. Only nothing is the same as it was."

"I don't get it."

Jules looked thoroughly confused, but then, so was Cammie. "I don't understand why, but I'm strongly attracted to him." She decided to hold off on sharing the rest of the story. Since she and Curt would never kiss again, what was the point?

"You are?" Her face a mask of wonder, Jules shook her head. "My best friend and my boyfriend's brother. Wow. Maybe we can double date."

Cammie clamped her lips together. "I don't want to date Curt Blanco," she said, keeping her voice low. "And I certainly don't want to be attracted to him. I'm looking for a man to settle down with and have babies, remember? Curt wants a woman to fool around with for a few weeks, and then more of the same. Dating him would be wrong and a waste of my time. That's something he and I both agree on."

To her surprise, Jules scoffed. "You've always been a Goody Two-shoes. A fling with Curt wouldn't hurt you one bit. Besides, if you two slept together, maybe Steven would take the hint and climb into bed with me."

"Did you not hear a word I said?" Cammie huffed in frustration. "Why did I even bother to say anything?"

But Jules's attention was focused on something over Cammie's shoulder. "Speak of the devil."

Cammie glanced behind her in time to see Kit and Eric Blanco stroll through the door, followed by Curt and Steven. Throughout the room, heads turned—but then, the handsome Blanco men were hard to ignore.

Cammie groaned. "He's the last person I wanted to see this morning."

"Speak for yourself. There aren't any booths or tables available, so let's invite them to share ours." Before Cammie could say, "This table is only big enough for four, so no, thank you," Jules tossed her head, curled her lips into an alluring smile, and did everything but shout to draw Kit and the Blanco brothers to the table.

OF ALL THE LUCK, CURT THOUGHT as he squeezed a chair between Cammie and Eric. There wasn't room anyplace else around the table. Who'd have guessed Rosy's would be so busy with tourist season not even in full swing, or that Cammie and Jules would be here?

Steven's latest squeeze had invited him and the rest of the family to share their table. Since there was nothing else available and since Steven was crazy for Jules, Curt was stuck.

He glanced at his older brother, who wore a goofy grin and couldn't take his eyes off Jules, and mentally threw up his hands. So much for deciding what to do about their father.

As Curt sat down, his chair bumped Cammie's. She threw him a dirty look, then made a show of scooting closer to Kit, who was sitting at the corner of the table.

"There's not much room," he said by way of apologizing. And wondered how he could get out of this.

"What are you doing here?" she murmured, and she wasn't smiling.

As unhappy about this as Cammie, he frowned. "We eat here almost every Saturday." They'd started the tradition right after their father's accident. "Believe me, if I'd known you were here, I'd have stayed home."

"You two sound like little kids," Eric said. "Why don't you kiss and make up or something?"

They'd done that. And how. Unwilling to go near that subject, Curt let Cammie do the explaining.

"What with the volleyball league and various events we're both working, we can't seem to get away from each other," she said, sounding as irritated as he felt.

"You used to like spending time together," Kit pointed out.

That was before their relationship had taken a turn toward hot and bothered. Curt clamped his jaw shut, and Cammie fiddled with her empty juice glass.

"So that's how it is," Steven said. "Life would be easier if you'd make up and be friends again."

Jules arched her eyebrows. "Oh, they have."

The sharp look Cammie shot her made Curt wonder exactly what Jules knew.

Eric and Kit exchanged surprised looks. "We hadn't heard," Eric said.

"It only happened last night," Curt said, shrugging.

In the close quarters, his shoulders nudged Cammie's. Their thighs brushed. His body stirred, which really miffed him, and the hunger he'd experienced last night flared again. He stifled a groan.

For damn sure he wasn't about to share the rest of what had happened between him and Cammie—those red-hot kisses or the night he'd suffered through, aching and frustrated for a woman he was totally wrong for. Fantasizing about her was worse than playing with matches near gasoline. Nothing but misery would come from that. Yet here he was, all but salivating and on the verge of a hard-on.

He sensed rather than saw her flush, and knew that she, too, was remembering last night. But unlike him, this morning she wasn't thinking about the unbelievable chemistry between them. She was ticked.

Eyes narrowed, Steven glanced from Curt to Cammie and back to Curt. "You aren't acting like you made up."

Rosy appeared with coffee for the newcomers and a concerned expression. "Much as I enjoy the Blanco family, this table isn't big enough for everyone. I'm sure something will open up soon."

Great news. Curt started to rise, but none of the rest of his family did. He gave up and settled in his seat.

"We don't mind squeezing together," Steven said, smiling at Jules. Who beamed right back. If she got any closer she'd be on his lap.

Rosy laughed. "I can see that." She homed in on Curt. A crafty gleam filled her eyes, and she nodded at Cammie. "You didn't tell me you and Curt made up. Maybe you should think about dating him."

With an unhappy moan, Cammie buried her face in her hands. Every person at the table, and some from other tables and booths turned to stare.

"I warned you," Jules murmured to Cammie.

"Cammie and I are friends, period," he stated good and loud, for everyone's benefit.

Cammie straightened and nodded. "And only on a trial basis."

Yesterday that had felt right, but after last night their friendship truly had become a trial for Curt. Much as he wanted to resume the easy camaraderie of before, unless his body settled down, that wasn't happening.

"Friendship is something at least," Rosy said. "Just don't go fixing her up with a jerk like Todd again."

While he sat there, smarting over that, she went on. "You want your usual steak, two eggs, sunny-side up, and English muffins with extra butter?"

Not about to open his mouth again, he nodded.

And silently planned to eat and run, regardless of what the rest of his family wanted.

SITTING THIGH TO THIGH BESIDE Curt brought back the heated feelings of last night. Cammie held herself stiff and aloof, but as Rosy took the orders from the Blancos, she also counted her blessings. At least she had a decent excuse for leaving soon. Kelly was picking her up in an hour, and she needed to get home and finish packing.

Jules shot her a curious glance. Eyes narrowed in warning, Cammie gave her head a fractional shake. Her friend nodded, and Cammie knew that at last she understood. Lusting after Curt was no joke.

"What'd you decide about your dad?" Jules asked, focusing on Steven.

Cammie noted the suddenly somber faces around her, Curt included. "Did something else happen to him?"

"He's holding his own," Curt replied. "But his legs still aren't working right, and the pain has gotten worse. He might need more surgery, and then follow-up physical therapy. Or he could up his current level of physical therapy from three times a week to daily and see what happens. Pop says he doesn't want more surgery, but we figured we should discuss the matter anyway."

"Then we'll leave you to it," Cammie said, glancing at Jules.

"No reason you can't listen in." Steven touched Jules's cheek. "Stay a while longer."

She smiled into his eyes. "Okay."

Since Cammie had caught a ride with Jules, she was stuck. "Only for a little while," she said. "I have plans today, and I need to get home soon."

She couldn't read Curt's expression, but thought she saw relief there. He wanted her to leave as badly as she did. The knowledge gave her no comfort.

"I'm sorry about your father," she said. "If he does have this operation, will it be the last one?"

"The surgery should help relieve the pressure on his back and make it easier to walk," Curt replied, "but there's no guarantee."

Eric nodded. "Adding more physical therapy could work just as well."

"But Dr. Scheyer, the neurosurgeon, is optimistic about the surgery," Kit added. "He hasn't steered the family wrong yet."

"Whether Pop goes the surgery route or increases his PT, we need a small fortune," Steven said. "He should've bought extra insurance," he added, looking straight at Cammie—her parents could have sold him the added coverage—"but he never figured on mangling his body in a car accident."

"Never thought he'd get older, either," Curt said.

Tucking her shoulder-length brown hair behind her ears, Kit glanced from Cammie to Jules. "In case you two don't realize this, Blanco men seem to believe they're invincible. They're bullheaded that way," she said, taking the edge off the words with a loving smile at her husband.

Eric rolled his eyes. "Listen babe, I've got plenty of insurance coverage. If anything happens to me, I don't want you, Curt or Steven putting in the overtime we all are now."

Kit looked alarmed. "Nothing's going to happen to you."

"Now who's unrealistic?" Eric teased. "I will get old. We all will."

"Enough of this morbid subject," Steven said in a forceful tone no one could ignore.

Jules showered him with an adoring smile. "Before we branched off into depressing topics, where were we?"

"Staring at each other."

Curt's brother returned the love-struck grin. He and Jules looked utterly happy. Cammie's heart ached with envy.

Within seconds, Steven and Jules seemed to have forgotten everyone else. Lost in their own world, they bent their heads together and murmured in low, intimate tones for their ears only.

Cammie hoped with every fiber in her being that Steven didn't break her best friend's heart—or vice versa. "If you decide your dad needs that operation, are you getting enough extra work to help pay for it?" she asked Curt.

"Doing my best," he said. "Like Eric said, we all are."

"We're sure glad Weston Atwood hired Curt to shoot his daughter's wedding," Eric said. He glanced at Cammie. "You and Curt used to be a hell of a great combo. Now that you're friends again… Any extra work you toss his way would be much appreciated."

"Mind your own business," Curt muttered.

Rosy arrived with their food, distracting everyone.

Everything smelled heavenly. Despite having finished her oatmeal, Cammie wanted more. Her mouth watered and her stomach rumbled.

Curt tucked into his breakfast as if he hadn't eaten for days. He ate with great gusto, which was fun to watch. Despite eating whatever he wanted, whenever he wanted it, the lucky man didn't have much fat on him, either. Mostly hard muscle.

He must have heard her wayward stomach. Swallowing a mouthful, he nodded at his side plate of English muffins. "Take one."

"No, thanks."

"When we were friends, you used to steal from my plate all the time. I don't mind."

"She's watching her figure," Rosy said. "So she can attract a new man."

Cammie's face warmed and she knew she was blushing. She didn't say anything though, for fear of what Rosy might pop up with next.

"What's wrong with your figure?" Curt asked, his gaze assessing her from her shoulders to her thighs—all that he could see while sitting at the table.

Acutely self-consciousness, she pulled in her stomach and straightened her shoulders.

"Like I told you at the Bar and Grill a few weeks ago, you look great," he murmured in a low, suggestive voice that put her nerves on alert.

Without intending to, she smiled. Then caught herself and sobered.

Rosy shook her head. "You sure you two aren't interested in dating?"

"That's my opinion, as a *friend*." Curt dipped his head and returned to his food.

"Okay," Rosy said. "Signal if you need anything." She hurried off.

"Cammie and Kelly are going to the dressmaker's in Portland," Jules said. "Cammie thinks she should be thinner."

Kit looked puzzled. "Surely by now, Kelly has her dress."

"What does Kelly's dress have to do with Cammie's body?" Curt asked after swallowing his mouthful.

"It's *my* dress we're having made," Cammie explained. She glanced at her watch. "We're leaving in less than an hour. In fact, if I don't get home and finish packing, I won't be ready when she picks me up. So if you don't mind, Jules…"

"I *do* mind." Jules pursed her lips into a pout. "I want to stay here with Steven." She angled her chin Curt's way. "Could you give her a ride?"

"That's up to Cammie," he said, but his cheerless expression conveyed his feelings.

He no more wanted to give her a ride than she wanted him to. And she was going to shoot Jules later.

She glared at her friend. "Can't you drop me off and come back?"

Jules gave a reluctant nod. "I suppose I—"

"I'll do it," Curt said. "Just let me finish eating."

Chapter Seven

As Curt and Cammie headed for the door, customers turned to stare. Curt nodded at Andy Jessup and Sharon Mahoney and Sharon's daughter, Abby, Cranberry's math whiz and a fun kid to photograph.

"I appreciate this," Cammie said. "And I'm sorry about rushing your breakfast."

"No problem." He shrugged. "Giving you a ride when you need it—that's what friends are for."

Her grateful expression made him glad he'd scarfed down his food.

"But what about your family meeting?"

"It'll keep." He opened the heavy glass door and they exited the diner.

A fine spring rain misted the air, and as they headed for Curt's car two blocks down the street, Cammie touched her hair.

"I didn't think to bring a rain hat. My hair," she wailed, raising her purse over her head.

Her giant handbag did protect her from the rain, but not the mist, and within seconds her hair reverted to its natural state. Curt thought she looked cute in corkscrews and frizz, but knew better than to say so.

"Come on," he said, sprinting for his car.

He unlocked the doors. Breathing hard, they slid into their seats. Traffic was busier than during the off-season but normal for this time of year, and he couldn't pull out right away. As he waited to nose into the street, Cammie pulled down the visor, frowned into the mirror, and worked her fingers through her hair. Which didn't do a thing to tame it.

Heaving a defeated sigh, muttering about straightening it again before Kelly picked her up, she snapped the visor closed.

The rain intensified. Curt adjusted the wipers, then joined the parade of cars on the street.

"Sometimes I wonder about Jules," Cammie said.

"Sometimes I wonder about Steven. I mean, I can understand sexual attraction." Hell, wasn't Curt fighting the same damn thing for Cammie right now? "But I don't get the love stuff at all." The truck in front of him signaled, and he slowed down. Then shook his head. "And I sure as hell wonder how Steven can fall in love again, after two painful divorces."

"Some people are willing to try until they find the right partner."

Cammie was. She wanted love and marriage so much, she seemed ready to forget how Todd had hurt her and put her trust in some other guy. Curt only hoped that the man, whoever he turned out to be, held that trust sacred. If he broke her heart, Curt would personally murder him.

With a faraway look on her face, Cammie sighed. "Who knows, Jules and Steven could be together forever."

Slowing for Cranberry's one traffic light, which had turned yellow, Curt snorted. "You're kidding, right?

Steven is a Blanco, and sooner or later, he and Jules will split up. When they do, I'll be here to pick up the pieces, dust off my brother and push him forward, until he screws up again with some other woman."

God knew, he'd been very supportive of both his brothers. They'd never had to prop him up though, and they would never have to. He was too smart to dive into that type of agony. Love hurt and he wanted none of it.

Cammie looked sad at the thought. "I hope you're wrong."

The light turned green, and Curt sped forward. Where Cammie saw romance, happy endings and white picket fences, he saw the misery of relationships turned sour. Their outlooks on life were as different as night and day, a good reminder that they were all wrong for each other—no matter how badly he wanted her.

He glanced her way, but she was staring out her window and he couldn't see her face. He did have a great view of her slender neck. Even that turned him on. A certain part of him stirred to life. Unfortunately he wanted her one hell of a lot. Frowning, he shifted in his seat.

Once they left downtown, traffic eased. Out Curt's window the beach was deserted and the ocean looked gray and churning. On Cammie's side, shrubs, trees and houses lined the road. Her cottage was a half mile farther down, on the wooded side.

"What's on your agenda today?" she asked.

Aside from taking an icy shower to cool off? "At some point I'll probably hit the gym and shoot hoops a while." Physical fatigue helped tamp down a man's lust, too. "But first there's a meeting at Weston's. He's on my case to see the negatives and proofs from that first meeting at the Oceanside and last week's dinner."

"I can't wait to see them, either, but what's the rush? The wedding isn't for another four weeks."

"You know Weston. He wants everything yesterday."

"Are they even ready yet?" Cammie asked, looking worried.

He rounded a bend in the road and her yellow clapboard house with its dark green shutters came into view. He signaled and slowed down. "According to last night's voice mail, the color stuff is." Developing color film was a toxic process better handled by a lab. "I'll pick up the negatives, then stop by the *Weekly News* and use their darkroom to develop the black-and-white proofs," he added as he turned into her blacktop driveway.

"Black-and-white?" Cammie shot him a surprised look. "That doesn't sound like Weston. But it does set a romantic tone."

"Exactly," Curt said. "And the depth and quality are unmatchable. I'm betting he'll like them."

"He just might. When do I get to see the proofs? And what about Kelly and Rick? It's their wedding."

"Weston wants control, and since he's footing the bills…"

"That figures," Cammie muttered. "I'm sure he'll be pleased. After all, you are the best."

Except for the time Weston had forced her, she hadn't complimented him since before calling off her own wedding. The praise felt good, and Curt's chest swelled. "Let's hope." Pulling beside the detached garage, he braked to a stop.

"Got a date tonight?" she asked, shooting him a sideways glance.

Tough to focus on someone else when Cammie was the woman he wanted. He shook his head. And swore she looked relieved.

"Thanks for the ride." She opened her door.

"Stay dry, and have fun in Portland."

She dashed from the car to her porch, ducking under the eaves while she unlocked the door. Curt waited until she waved and hurried inside before backing his car into the small turnaround.

He drove off wanting her so much, he ached.

It was a good thing she was leaving town. Out of sight, out of mind, and he intended to push her out of his head once and for all. Starting now.

"USE EITHER FITTING ROOM," said Mrs. Nevers, the plump, middle-aged seamstress who was making dresses for Cammie and everyone in Kelly's wedding. "I'll be in shortly." She turned to Kelly. "I want to show you the netting I found."

"Oh, boy," Kelly said. She waved at Cammie. "Be back soon."

Excited, Cammie pulled the curtain across the opening of the small fitting room. She'd never hired a dressmaker to custom-design an outfit. This would be fun, even if the cost would be more than she'd ever paid for a dress. This was Kelly. To make her wedding day the best it could be, Cammie was willing to pay a fortune.

Taking care not to mess up her hair, which she'd straightened twice today, she eased her cotton knit dress over her head.

Mrs. Nevers returned with a tape measure and a stubby pencil. Self-conscious in her white cotton bra and bikini panties, Cammie stood still while the dressmaker measured her breasts, hips, the distance between her shoulders and hips and other places, pausing between each measurement to jot down the information on a sheet of paper.

After she finished and exited into the showroom, Cammie dressed. She could hear the low voices of Mrs. Nevers and Kelly, but couldn't make out what they were saying. Eager to find out, she smoothed her hair, which looked satisfyingly neat, then opened the curtain.

"I see her in a three-piece outfit—skirt, jacket and blouse that emphasizes her hourglass figure," Mrs. Nevers was saying. She gestured with her hands. "Like so."

"Okay." Gaze narrowed and focused as if she could see the dressmaker's vision in her mind, Kelly tapped her index finger to her lips. "Cammie has great legs. We want something that shows them off, too."

While Cammie gaped at her younger friend, who suddenly sounded so decisive and grown-up, Mrs. Nevers gave a thoughtful nod. Taking an artist's pad from the cluttered desk in the corner, she quickly sketched a design.

Cammie and Kelly studied it. "I like this," Kelly said. "What do you think, Cammie?"

Feeling out of her element, Cammie offered a weak smile. "I wish I could say, 'I love this,' but I can't quite picture myself in it. I trust the two of you."

"Excellent." Mrs. Nevers nodded. "I'll make up a muslin prototype for you to try on." She glanced at her watch. "It's two-thirty now. Can you come back at four-thirty?"

"Wow." Cammie's eyes widened. "That's fast."

"That's why I love Mrs. N.," Kelly said, shooting a fond grin at the dressmaker. "She's fast and very good."

The bell over the door rang as they exited. "She's also charging enough to make the rush worth her while," Kelly murmured when they reached the sidewalk.

"Considering we only have a few weeks before the wedding, that's understandable," Cammie said. The air here was warmer than in Cranberry, and she turned her face toward the sun. "What shall we do while we wait?"

"That's easy." Kelly dug into her purse and pulled out a platinum credit card. "Daddy gave me this to get some clothes for my trousseau. Let's go shopping."

Two hours later, the trunk of Kelly's car bulging with packages, Cammie stood before a triple mirror in Mrs. Nevers's showroom and studied herself. The muslin prototype designed for her body included a pencil skirt cut to an inch above the knee with two side slits, and a fitted jacket that flared slightly at the hip. Her waist looked tiny and her legs looked long. She didn't have a blouse prototype, as Mrs. Nevers hadn't had time to make that.

She met Kelly's eye in the mirror. "What do you think?"

"It shows off your legs and figure perfectly. Sophisticated and flattering... I love it!" She threw the dressmaker a thumbs-up. "Mrs. N., you're a genius."

The dressmaker beamed. "The blouse will be beautiful, too."

"And when she makes the real thing..." Kelly whistled. "Look out single men everywhere."

Cammie smiled at the thought. She wondered what Curt would think of her outfit. Caught herself and frowned.

What did his opinion matter? He wasn't the man she wanted to attract—he was her friend.

"What fabric and color did you have in mind?" she asked.

"Deep rose moiré silk taffeta to match the rose trim of the bridesmaid dresses. With your pale skin and blond hair the color will be stunning. The blouse will be made from the finest China silk and a shade lighter." Mrs. Nevers held up a finger. "Wait, I have samples in the back."

She brought out two squares of fabric and a hand mirror. Cammie held each square to her face and studied her reflection. "It does make my skin look nice," she commented.

"Nice?" Kelly said. "You'll be radiant. We only have three weeks. When will it be ready for fitting?"

Face scrunched, Mrs. Nevers looked at the white plaster ceiling, seeming to calculate in her head. "The wedding gown will be ready ten days from now. I should be able to finish Cammie's suit by then, too. If you don't mind, I'll do both final fittings on the same day."

Cammie could hardly wait to see Kelly's dress and her suit. She pulled her BlackBerry from her purse and punched in the appointment.

"What about the bridesmaids?" Kelly asked.

"They're coming later this week."

"Are you sure that's enough time?" Cammie asked.

"I don't normally work so quickly." Mrs. Nevers shrugged. "But for Kelly…"

"I really appreciate that," Kelly said. "See you in ten days."

She and Cammie walked out, the bell over the door

ringing and the spring sky pale as the sun sank toward the horizon.

Exuberant, Cammie hugged Kelly. "This is such fun!"

When she and Kelly let go of each other, Kelly's eyes were wet. "Thanks for being such a great friend all these years. I love you like a sister."

"Me, too." Cammie's eyes filled, too. They both sniffled, then laughed.

"You ready for dinner?" Cammie asked. "Or would you rather shop some more?"

"Shopping, please," Kelly said. "We both need shoes."

"Sounds good. Let's get our shoes, then have dinner and maybe catch a movie."

"Great minds think alike," Kelly said. "Oh, and tonight is on me."

"You should be saving your money for after you're married," Cammie advised, sounding to her own ears like a mother hen. Stodgy, even. Jules had called her a Goody Two-shoes. The very thought caused her to cringe. "Do you think I'm stuffy?"

Kelly angled an assessing look her way. "You want the truth?" At Cammie's nod, she shrugged. "A little."

That rankled. Cammie lifted her chin. "I don't dress that way, and I certainly don't feel it."

"Your clothes are cute," Kelly agreed. "But your attitude seems...prissy."

"It does?" Cammie groaned. "If that's true I'll never attract a man. I want to be sexy and alluring."

"It all boils down to perception," Kelly said, sounding wise and mature for the second time today. "If you feel sexy, you'll act sexy."

"Just how do I do that?"

"Well…" Kelly looked pensive. "Do you own any hot underwear?"

Cammie thought dismally of her mostly utilitarian cotton panties and bras. "Not really."

"Why not buy yourself something slinky and sexy?" Kelly winked. "To bring out the hidden you."

"Now, there's an idea." Pleased with the simple solution, Cammie grinned. "You may be seven years younger than I am, but you sure are smart."

"Thank you." Kelly curtsied. "What do you say we shop for shoes *and* underwear?"

"I say, yes," Cammie said.

"As a smart woman, may I also point out that you just spent a fortune on an outfit for my wedding. Treating you to dinner and a movie is the least I can do. Besides…" Kelly leaned in close and lowered her voice. "It's not really my money tonight—it's Daddy's."

"I'm not sure he'd want you to treat me," Cammie argued.

"He won't mind."

He'd probably have a fit. "Lately he seems to think I'm nothing more than the hired help."

"I hate when Daddy does that."

Kelly's mouth tightened, and for a moment she was the image of her father. In some ways she was a lot like him, Cammie realized.

"He's such a control freak," Kelly continued, "and he's driving me crazy. Do you know, he expects me to call him later, and tell him what I bought? Knowing Daddy, if he doesn't approve of my purchases, he'll make me return them." Her jaw set. "As if. I have to do *something* without his stamp of approval, so will you please let me treat you to dinner and a movie?"

"Okay," Cammie said, giving in. "But I want you to remember something, Kelly. Your father adores you, and his actions are borne out of love. Not every woman is so lucky. Or has a father who likes the man she wants to marry."

Kelly looked surprised, as if she'd never considered this. "I suppose you're right. Thanks for reminding me. I guess I will call Daddy later and tell him what I bought." She sighed. "The truth is, as long as Rick and I are together and married, I'm happy. Nothing else really matters."

Cammie envied her younger friend. "You're lucky, Kelly. You found your soul mate early in life."

"You'll find the right guy, too, Cammie. I know it. Now, let's go shopping."

IN THE DARKROOM of the deserted *Cranberry News,* Curt examined his black-and-white proofs. They were every bit as good as the color proofs from the lab.

Especially the pictures of Cammie that day at the Oceanside. Those, Weston would never see. Cammie, either. No telling what she'd think. Curt had captured her perfectly, from the twin puckers between her brows and less-than-pleased look in her eyes—she'd still been mad at him then—to her cute nose and slightly compressed lips. The tiny mole high on her right cheek added to her charm. Even frowning, she was beautiful, as photogenic as any model.

He liked the close-ups of her torso, too. The white blouse and short, V-neck pullover outlined her pert breasts, and her short, pleated skirt revealed the curve of her womanly hips. And those shapely legs…

Oh, yeah. Nothing wrong with Cammie's body. She was about as perfect as a woman could be, and he still didn't get why she thought she should lose weight.

He turned an assessing gaze to the last row of the Cammie proofs, which showcased the tattoo over her ankle. She had great ankles, too. In one shot her legs were crossed at the knee, and her pump dangled from her toes. The arch of her foot was pronounced, and for some reason, sexy as hell.

His groin stirred. He let out a frustrated groan.

Out of sight, out of mind, remember? He slipped the Cammie sheets into a large envelope and fastened the clip on the back. He would take them home and stash them in a file.

Distraction removed, he turned his attention to the other proof pages taken at the Oceanside. Weston had insisted on smiling for the camera, but on his face the genial expression looked posed and as phony as a desert sunset in Cranberry. Without a bulldog scowl in sight, he'd no doubt be pleased.

The photos of Rick and Kelly were much better. Their love was a palpable thing, and each picture recorded their candid, adoring glances and caught the electricity between them. As happy as they seemed, Curt couldn't stop a cynical smirk. Love never lasted, and he wouldn't be surprised if they split up in a few years.

The proofs from the dinner party showed more of Kelly and Rick, sometimes less than happy. But then, Weston had hounded them nonstop. There were a few good shots of Cammie and plenty of the guests, smiling, talking, eating and drinking. The images of Weston were less posed—lording over all, his shrewd eyes missing nothing.

Not exactly flattering, but they captured the real essence of the man. He wasn't going to like this batch. As Curt debated over whether to trash the worst shots, the alarm on his watch beeped, reminding him that he was due at the Atwood home.

With little time to spare, he gathered all the page proofs and slid them into the expensive leather folio he used for clients. He grabbed the envelope of Cammie proofs and headed out.

Forty-five minutes later, he sat opposite Weston's expansive desk at his large home office while his boss scrutinized the shots.

"I like both the color and black-and-white pictures of me at the dinner party," he said. "The ones from the Oceanside stink."

Wondering whether he'd heard right, Curt scratched his head. "Let me get this straight—you like these—" he leaned forward and pointed to images of Weston wearing his trademark I-am-in-charge scowl "—but not the ones of you smiling."

Weston nodded. "Those are crap, and you should have warned me when you took them."

As if he would have listened. Curt bit back an oath.

"I want them changed to look like the real me."

Altering nondigital pictures was expensive, time-consuming and a pain in the butt and went against Curt's artistic grain. He frowned. "You didn't want digital, remember? With regular film, changes aren't that easy without a reshoot and careful splicing."

"Ask me if I care." Weston set his jaw. "Set up the shoot and fix those pictures."

"Don't you want to talk to Kelly and Cammie first?"

"It's my money." Weston drew his bushy brows together. "I make the decisions."

Curt knew the mulish man would not budge. "It'll cost you," he warned.

"Not if you want to shoot this wedding. There are other photographers who'd happily take over."

Though Curt couldn't afford to lose the job, he refused to bow down to the threat or pay for his boss's vanity. "None as good as I am. If these pictures were defective, I'd gladly cover the cost of a retake. But there's not a thing wrong with them." He looked at his boss straight on. "If you want reshoots, you'll pay for them."

His face mottled and red, Weston swore. Then he threw up his hands. "All right, Blanco, you win this round. But you better watch your mouth. Now, when can we reshoot?"

If Curt had had his camera he'd have done the job right then. "How about tomorrow morn—"

The phone rang, cutting him off. Gesturing at Curt to stay put, Weston picked up.

Curt thought about calling Cammie and telling her about their client's latest demand. Then he remembered—he didn't want to talk to her. Out of sight, out of mind, he reminded himself again.

"Hi, honey," Weston said in a warm, fatherly voice. "Kelly," he mouthed to Curt. "Curt's here and we're looking at proofs. I don't like the ones of me so he'll reshoot those." Kelly said something and he shook his head. "You won't have to be there. Curt's going to splice my

picture into yours. No, you'll see 'em after they're fixed."
Pausing, he listened. "You did?" A grin lit his face, and
his gaze shot to Curt. "She and Cammie bought their
shoes. Uh-huh," he said, still smiling into the phone.

The image Curt had taken of Cammie with one shoe
dangling from her toes popped into his mind. Damned
if his body didn't stir. He frowned. Out of sight, out of
mind wasn't working.

He was in bad shape and in need of a diversion. A fun-
loving woman would do the trick. He decided to stop by
the Bar and Grill on the way home and look around.

Only his car didn't cooperate. He drove straight home,
dropped the envelope of Cammie proofs on his desk for
later filing and took his second cold shower of the day.

That didn't work, either.

Chapter Eight

"Tell me again why you're wasting that gorgeous underwear on a volleyball game?" Jules asked as she, Cammie and a group of women headed from the girls' locker room into the gym on Tuesday night. "I get the point of changing into them *after* the game. But playing the first game of the season? On the soccer field?" She made a face. "They'll get all sweaty and dirty."

Marcy and several other women, who had admired the skimpy purple satin, lace-trimmed bra and panty set, moved in to hear Cammie's reply.

"Believe me, wearing nice undies now is not a waste," she assured them. Dressed in a lime-green T-shirt and matching shorts, she *looked* the same as always, but underneath, she *felt* incredibly sexy. With six new sets of equally sensuous underwear at home—she'd laid them across her bed to admire—she intended to feel this way all the time. No more stuffy behavior for her. "*I* know what I'm wearing, and that's enough."

"Ah," Marcy said, comprehension dawning on her face. "You mean you know that under those clothes you look like a sex goddess and it'll shine through."

Cammie nodded. "Bingo."

"Not a bad idea," Janey, Marcy's best friend, commented. "Be sure and let us know how it works."

"Just who are you trying to attract?" Marcy asked.

Jules eyed her shrewdly. "Yes, who?"

The sixty-four-million-dollar question. Unable to stop herself, Cammie sought out Curt, who was talking to his brothers and several other men across the gym. Why he drew her attention, she couldn't have said.

She hadn't seen him since Saturday morning, and now... Her heart lifted. He must have sensed her appreciative stare, for his gaze jumped to hers. Cammie could see the dark intensity in those eyes clear across the room. Unfortunately, despite her best intentions she was still more than attracted to him, and her body tingled. Flushing, she jerked her attention to the curious women around her. She fervently hoped her new sexy self would draw masculine interest from men who would take her mind off Curt once and for all.

"Let's just say, I have my eye on several prospects." She winked, which was completely unlike her. Proof that already the underwear was changing her.

"Well, my eyes are for one man only," Jules murmured. She smoothed down her snug T-shirt and wet her lips. "I'll see you ladies later."

She still hadn't lured Steven into bed, but she seemed less upset than she'd been at breakfast Saturday morning. Over the weekend, she'd told Cammie, she'd decided that with or without sex, Steven was worth hanging on to. A big change in attitude, but not surprising. Most men were putty in Jules's capable hands, and Steven's insistence that they wait to make love presented exactly the challenge that would hold her attention. That and the fact that she was in love with the man.

The other women headed for their respective teams. Marcy and Cammie fell into step. "Still dating Billy?" Cammie asked.

"No," Marcy said with a casual wave of her hand. "We got tired of each other. I'm ready to move on to someone else." She shot Cammie a sly look. "I think I'll try your plan and wear sexy undies to the game Thursday night."

"You already ooze sex appeal."

"Do I? Thanks." Marcy gestured toward Jules and Steven, who were talking earnestly, as if they were the only two people in the gym. "So do they."

Cammie could almost see the air vibrate between them. Though she longed for the same thing, tonight she observed them without a pang of envy. With the boost in self-confidence gained from wearing sexy underwear, she knew without a doubt that she would find and attract the perfect man for her.

"You look different," Curt said as he and Billy joined her and Marcy.

"I do?" Cammie gave her head a flirty shake. "How so?"

"I don't know." His eyes combed over her with warm appreciation. "Just different."

Marcy raised her brows at Cammie. "Is that good or bad?" she asked, eyeing Curt.

"Hot," Billy said.

Curt scowled at the other man, but didn't dispute the comment.

Wonder of wonders, it was working! Cammie made a mental note to kiss Kelly, who had pushed her to buy seven new sets of underwear and had urged her to wear them daily.

They joined the rest of their teammates and the two extra players, one male, one female, who had signed up late and rotated in during practice and games. Ten feet away, the Scorpions, the team they were playing tonight, waved and hooted, then disappeared through the exit, no doubt to head for the soccer field.

"Let's go trounce those guys," Mike said as he hustled them out.

Tonight the wind was soft, and the May air unusually mild. Though thanks to an afternoon downpour, the ground was soggy. Which meant that Cammie likely would end up wet and muddy. She questioned the wisdom of wearing her expensive underwear after all.

The two teams walked to the well-lit field and took their places, Cammie, who to her own amazement was good at spiking the ball over the net, in the middle front between Curt and Billy. Mike, Marcy and James Dawson, a tall, skinny guy who worked in shipping and receiving at the cranberry factory, stood in the back. On the opposite side of the net, Janey, an accountant named Rachael, and four very attractive single males took their positions. Four stand-ins, two men and two women, stood at the side to watch and cheer.

Cammie studied each man, wondering whether he might be her Mr. Right. Derek Jensen, the first server, was awfully cute. He was a lawyer, which meant he was smart, too. And a great player. Hmm…

The ball skimmed over the net. James passed it to Billy, who set it for Cammie. She spiked it over the net, catching the Scorpions by surprise. She'd scored the first point! She raised her fist. "Wahoo!"

Her teammates applauded her.

"Good hit," Curt said, his face filled with praise and admiration.

And his smile… Lordy. Her insides went haywire and her heart seemed to expand. She hid her reaction under a sportsmanlike nod. "Thanks."

Mike served for the Big Time Players. The teams volleyed the ball back and forth until the Scorpions scored.

"Point," Janey called out, looking smug and pleased.

"Good volleying, people," Mike encouraged. "This time, let's stop 'em."

Both teams rotated clockwise, putting Billy in the back, Cammie in right front, and Curt in the middle. Ben Gaiser, a cute computer geek who was seriously involved with Rachael, prepared to serve for the Scorpions. Desperate to move her focus off Curt, Cammie eyed Derek, who now stood front left. With his hands up, his T-shirt rose above his belly, and she caught a glimpse of his compact abs. Though he was exceptionally well built, she felt only mild admiration, nothing like the intense attraction for Curt. As the ball headed toward her, she pressed her lips together and prepared to pass the ball to James or Marcy. Maybe if she took the time to—

"Got it!" Curt said.

"Mine!" Billy called out at the same time.

Both men lunged for the ball. Cammie jumped back to get out of their way. Or tried to. The ground was wet. Her shoe slipped, slowing her retreat. Eyes on the ball, Billy plowed into her, pushing her into Curt. Her forehead collided hard with his chin.

"Ow!" she cried.

"Ouch!" Curt said.

Billy gave a sheepish look. "Sorry."

"Time out!" Mike called, forming a T with his hands.

"You okay?" Curt asked, squinting at her.

Gingerly touching her forehead, she winced. "I think so. What about you?"

He worked his jaw, then grimaced. "I'll live. That's some hard head you've got."

"Don't we all know it," Billy quipped.

Everyone but Cammie and Curt laughed.

Looking concerned Mike glanced from one to the other. "Should I call in our alternates?"

"Not for me," Curt said.

Cammie shook her head. The movement hurt and she couldn't stop a whine of pain.

With an anxious frown, Curt peered at her forehead. "Maybe you should go to the emergency room."

That was a long drive. "I'll be fine," she said.

Mike took her arm and pulled her under a light. "Look at me." He stared into her eyes. "No concussion that I can see, but that's a nasty bump. Better go home and ice it." He glanced at Curt. "That jaw needs ice, too. Why don't you drive Cammie home?"

She didn't want or need a ride from Curt. "I'm fine," she repeated. "But I think I will go home. In my own car."

"Then I'll follow you, and make sure you get there safe and sound," Curt said.

An offer any friend would make. And as with any good friend, if he followed her home he'd probably want to come inside. Since she felt more than friendly toward him, that was dangerous.

She started to shake her head, then bit her lip instead. "You stay here and finish the game."

He opened his mouth to argue. "Our team needs you more than I do. Go, Big Time Players!" she shouted, pumping her fist skyward.

"Yeah!" her teammates returned.

That worked. "Okay." Curt nodded to Mike.

Mike signaled an alternate, a woman named Judy who taught second grade. She waved at Cammie and took her place.

"Let's play ball," Mike hollered.

"Bye, Cammie." "Take care." "Hope to see you Thursday," her teammates called out.

"Good luck everyone."

As she headed off the field, the game resumed.

A LITTLE OVER AN HOUR LATER, his jaw bruised and aching, Curt pulled into Cammie's driveway. The first game of the season was over, with the Big Time Players victorious. Instead of joining his teammates at the Cranberry Bar and Grill for a victory pitcher, he'd showered, dressed and headed straight for Cammie's.

He'd really clobbered her forehead. Worry hammered his gut, and he knew he wouldn't rest until he made sure she was okay. If she hadn't gone to bed yet. Light peeked between the living-room drapes, which meant she was still up. Curt parked. He exited the car, strode to the front door and pushed the buzzer.

The porch light flashed on. Cammie opened the door, her face registering surprise. "What are you doing here?"

She'd changed into a fuzzy yellow robe that fell to midcalf, and striped socks. One hand clutched an ice pack. Her bangs were damp and curly, and an angry purple bump marred her normally smooth forehead. No makeup, either. In other words, she was not at her best.

Yet dog that he was, he wondered what was under that robe. He shoved his hands into the pockets of his jeans. "I wanted to check on you and let you know the good news. We won."

"That's great about winning, but there's no need to check on me, Curt. I'm fine."

With her face pale and her eyes shadowed with pain, she didn't look fine. That concerned him. "Friends check in on each other," he said. "Aren't you gonna invite me in?"

"Um…" She hesitated, then backed up. "Okay, you can come in, but only for a few minutes. I was about to go to bed."

Bed. The very mention of the word piqued Curt's imagination. Years back he'd helped her move that bed, a queen-size mahogany piece that had been in her parents' house, without so much as a sexual thought. Now, though…

Refusing to go there, he stepped into the small entry and nodded at the ice pack. "Is that helping?"

"Not really," she said as she closed the door. Chin angled, she studied his bruised jaw. "That's an ugly bruise. Does it hurt?"

"Yeah. Got any extra ice?"

"If you don't mind a plastic bag and a dish towel. Come on."

He followed her through the colorful, cozy living room, past the small dining room and into her surprisingly roomy kitchen. The deep rose walls, hardwood floors and butter-color counter gave the room colorful warmth.

"Sit down," she said.

He took a seat at the kitchen table. "What if you *do* have a concussion?" he asked as she filled a bag with ice from the ice maker. "If you don't want to drive to the clinic, maybe you should give Doc a call," he said. Doc, a family doctor who was an institution in Cranberry, had snubbed the new clinic miles outside town to keep his downtown office open.

Cammie shook her head. "Mike looked at my eyes. He says I don't have a concussion."

"That was hours ago. Things could have changed."

The ice pack was ready, and she handed it to him. Instead he snagged her wrist. "Look at me."

The ice pack clattered onto the table. Her big, beautiful eyes stared into his, blue with tiny silver flecks. Both pupils were the same size. "Any nausea? Blurred vision?"

"Nope."

"Mike was right—you look okay," Curt said, releasing her wrist.

"Told you." She sat down opposite him, retrieved her ice pack from the table and cautiously pressed it to her forehead.

Following suit, Curt settled the ice against his jaw. The cold felt soothing. He glanced at Cammie. "We're a fine pair."

A smile twitched her lips. "We certainly are." An instant later, she sighed. "What a waste of underwear."

Certain he'd misunderstood, Curt gave her a puzzled look. "Waste of underwear? I'll probably regret asking this, but what exactly do you mean?"

"Nothing," Cammie said, her gaze darting away from his.

Now she really had him curious. "We're friends," he reasoned. "You can tell me anything."

"Not this." Her cheeks flushed crimson, adding color to her pale face. "Kelly says Weston hated the pictures of himself."

If she wanted to change the subject, fine by Curt. "Remember how he demanded photos of himself with that phony happy grin? When he saw the proofs he changed his mind."

"Some people just don't look natural with smiles on their faces." Cammie absently combed her fingers through her hair, steering clear of her bangs. Even so, she winced.

"You look like you could go for a couple of pain tablets," he said. "I could use some myself."

"I took two earlier, but they're not working. Help yourself. There's a bottle in the master bathroom, top shelf of the medicine cabinet. But you really don't have to stay," she said, the grateful look in her eyes at odds with her words.

"I don't mind. Now sit tight and I'll be back with that bottle."

He knew her house well. He strode though the living room, absently noting the usual pile of catalogs—she often ordered stuff for her business from them—on the coffee table. Without bothering to flip on the hallway light, he headed past a small powder room and Cammie's office to the bedroom at the far end.

The bedside table lamp was on, giving the room a soft glow. Since he'd last been here, she'd bought a new spread and matching curtains—bright, flowered, feminine things didn't suit his tastes. What snagged his attention were the array of bras and panties arranged on the bedspread. Bronze-color, dusky rose, ivory and black, each was tiny and lacy and silky. The prettiest, sexiest underwear he'd ever seen.

And enough to fuel a man's brain into overdrive. For a moment he forgot about his jaw and Cammie's forehead. He imagined her in a set of those little panties and bras. A certain part of his body began to wake up. Swallowing, he moved into the bathroom.

Where another matching set titillated him, this one purple and made of see-through lace. The bra and panties were damp and hung over the towel bar to dry, meaning she'd worn them recently. A strangled sound tore from his throat, and his snug jeans felt tighter still.

He was no randy kid, and he scowled as he opened the medicine cabinet. The pain reliever was right where she'd said, on the top shelf. What she hadn't mentioned was the half-empty wheel of birth control pills beside it.

So she still was on the pill. Or maybe they were left over from Todd. Either way, he was anxious to get out of there. He slammed the cabinet with extra force. Averting his eyes, he strode rapidly through the bedroom and headed toward the kitchen.

Cammie had filled two glasses of water. Now, noting the tightly closed lapels of her robe, he couldn't help wondering again what was under there. Was she wearing a lacy bra and skimpy panties?

Lust boiled inside him. As he quickly sat down, he thought wryly about shoving his ice pack a lot lower than his jaw.

If he were smart, he'd leave soon. He shook out two pain tablets for himself, then handed Cammie the bottle.

After they swallowed the pills, he opened his mouth to tell her good-night. "What's with the fancy underwear?" he asked instead.

"You saw them?"

"Since they're spread over your bed and hanging in the bathroom they were hard to miss." Emphasis on *hard*. He shifted uncomfortably.

Her turn to look uncomfortable. "I guess I forgot." Blushing and clutching her lapels in one hand, she cleared her throat. "So what are you doing about Weston's photos?"

For the life of him, he barely understood her. He kept picturing her in the see-through bra and sexy panties.

"Who'd you buy those things for?" he pushed, jealousy stirring.

"What things?"

"Those microscopic panties and bras."

Hearing the disapproval in his voice, she drew herself up straight. "Not that it's any of your business, but for myself."

The unexpected explanation baffled him speechless.

Cammie must have guessed at his confusion, for the tight pinch of her mouth eased. She set down her ice pack. "You wouldn't understand."

"Believe me, I want to. Try me."

She wasn't about to talk, so he pulled his trump card. "We used to tell each other everything. I thought we were friends again."

Remorse crossed her face and he knew he'd scored.

"All right, but I need your word that you won't repeat this to anyone," she said, sounding the way she used to when they'd been friends and nothing more.

Her trust felt good. Looking straight into her eyes, he nodded soberly. "I swear."

Another beat of hesitation while she set down the ice pack. "I haven't exactly been feeling attractive lately. Leftover anxiety from Todd, I guess."

Leaning toward him, collar gaping some to allow him a tantalizing view of the smooth skin below her neck, she sure as hell looked sexy. Even though he could see nothing beyond the small triangle of skin, it was enough to fuel his fantasies. And make him feel like a rat. Some friend he was.

"Kelly convinced me to buy sexy underwear so I'd feel better about myself," Cammie added. "So I'm trying it."

"You're trying it now?"

Catching her lip between her teeth, she nodded.

God almighty. He gripped his ice pack in his fist. "What color are they?" he said through clenched teeth.

Thankfully she didn't seem to notice. "Lilac with lace trim," she replied, demurely pulling her collar shut.

"Lilac, huh," he said, his imagination going wild. He set the ice pack on the table with a not-quite-steady hand. "Is it working? Do you feel sexy?"

"At volleyball practice, I did, but at the moment, no." She gestured at her forehead. "I'm sure I don't look it, either."

"You always look sexy to me. Even now." Unable to mask his need, he gazed hungrily at her.

Her eyes widened before she frowned at her ice pack. Curt swallowed an oath. She didn't want sexual interest from him, she wanted friendship. He really should leave now, before he did something he shouldn't and ruined everything.

But he could no more move than stop breathing. "A minute ago you asked what I'm doing about Weston," he said, striving to move to neutral ground. "He wants new photos I can splice into the existing shots. That wouldn't be a problem with digital film. But with regular film…" He shook his head.

"That man is such a pain," Cammie said, as if she truly believed they were friends and nothing more.

"I don't like it either, but I need the money."

"Speaking of money, what did you decide about your father? Is he having the operation?"

"He's fighting it, but we're working on him." They all were saving money as fast as they could so that he'd give in.

"Wish him well from me." Cammie leaned back in her chair. The collar of her robe opened a fraction. This time, Curt swore he saw a flash of lilac lace.

His body went on full alert. "Will do," he managed to say.

"The pain reliever is working at last," she said. "My head is starting to feel better."

"Same with the jaw." But Curt's head, the one between his legs, began to throb. He couldn't leave now if he wanted to. He cleared his throat. "Tell me about Portland."

"I've never been to a dressmaker before. It was fun," she said, and for the first time her eyes sparkled. "We go back next Tuesday for the final fitting. I'll have to miss volleyball."

"The team will survive. Will you be wearing your lilac underwear?" The words slipped out before he could stop them.

Cammie's startled gaze darted away, but not before he saw the impact of his words. *She knows I want her.* Now he'd gone and wrecked everything.

Hard-on or not, he was outta here. While he still could go. "It's getting late, and we both need rest." He pushed back his chair and stood.

Holding the ice pack to her forehead, Cammie, too, stood. Her sash was loose, and this time her robe gaped open. She dropped the ice pack and jerked it closed.

Too late. He'd seen the bra and the tiny slip of silk that barely covered her mound.

He cleared his throat. "You're right. You look sexy as hell in that underwear."

"Thank you. I think."

Her attention dropped to his groin. Her eyes widened. No man could miss that avid, lustful expression.

Looked as if she wanted him, too.

The last of his waning control snapped, along with common sense. Blood roaring in his head, he reached for her.

Chapter Nine

Don't do this, a voice in Cammie's head warned. But the hot look in Curt's eyes coupled with her own fierce yearning were impossible to fight. She closed her eyes, twined her arms around his neck and offered her lips.

The smells of soap and man invaded her senses before his mouth covered hers with an urgency she matched. She needed no coaxing to open her mouth or tangle her tongue with his.

It wasn't enough.

As if Curt read her mind, he fumbled with the sash on her robe. Eager to feel his hands on her body, panting, she broke the kiss and slipped out of the robe. Cool air washed over her fevered skin. She shivered, though not from the temperature.

Breathing hard, Curt studied her through eyes that smoldered with desire. "Beautiful."

"You really like it?"

"Oh, yeah."

The way he looked at her, with hunger and intense appreciation, made her feel womanly, sexy and grateful that she'd bought and worn the lilac set. His hooded gaze homed in on her breasts. Her nipples tightened as if he'd touched them. One finger traced the scalloped edge of her demibra, teasing without actually touching. "Damn, but you're fine."

Unable to bear one more instant of torture, she clasped his wrists and guided his palms to her breasts. "Touch me."

"Dear God." Groaning, Curt closed his eyes.

Through a haze of desire, Cammie watched his face. The awed expression alone flooded her with warmth. Then he cupped her through the lace. A shudder of pleasure shook her, and once again her eyelids fluttered shut. She let out a ragged breath, pushing against his skilled fingers.

Liquid heat shot to the throbbing nub between her legs. Her panties grew damp, and her legs threatened to buckle. "I don't think I can stand up one more second," she said.

"Me, either."

Grasping her hands, Curt backed into a kitchen chair. He sat down and pulled her sideways onto his lap. His arousal poked her bottom, making her want so much more.

Eyes dark with need, he gave her a fevered smile. "Now, where were we?"

"You were in the process of making me feel very good," she said.

"Touching you makes me feel great, too." His gaze dropped to her breasts. "Much as I like that pretty bra, it's got to come off."

Reaching behind her, he deftly undid the hooks. He slid the straps down her arms with trembling fingers. Or maybe she was the one trembling. Warm, moist breath bathed her nipple. Then his mouth closed over her. His tongue swept the sensitive tip. Whimpering, she wove her fingers through his hair and urged him closer.

While his hand cupped and kneaded her other breast, he suckled her. A moan of pleasure purled from her throat.

Curt, too, moaned. As if he were in pain.

"Does your jaw hurt?" she whispered.

"Not when I'm kissing you."

He turned his attention to the other breast and the waves of pleasure continued. Cammie shifted restlessly until she straddled him. She wriggled closer, pressing the aching place between her legs hard against his arousal. With very little more she would climax.

Curt gripped her hips and stilled her. "If you don't stop wriggling, I swear, I'll embarrass myself."

"I'm there, too," Cammie said. "I'll hold still if you take off your shirt."

She inched back. Curt pulled his rugby shirt over his head. His torso was muscled and beautiful, with a smattering of hair across his pecs. Eager to be closer, she wrapped her arms around his neck.

Curt hugged her tight, his arms solid and warm. The hair on his chest teased her nipples and his skin against hers felt like heaven. His body was taut and hard. Hot, eager hands roamed her back, then cupped her bottom, pulling her against his arousal.

"I thought you were worried about embarrassing yourself," she reminded him.

"I'll be all right as long as you're still. You feel so damn good," he murmured.

Her body pulsed and hummed. How she wanted him.

She knew she'd die if he didn't make love to her. Right now. Breathless, she broke away to look into his eyes. "Let's take off everything."

Curt froze, the desire in his eyes mixed with anguish. "Believe me, I want that more than I can say, but we can't make love." Looking soul deep into her eyes, he shifted her off his groin. "You want more than I can give. You know my track record, Cammie. I've never been able to stay with a woman for long. I leave her, she leaves me… It never works out."

Suddenly she was off his lap and he was on his feet. He plucked her robe and his shirt from the floor.

Refusing to take her robe, but crossing her arms over her breasts, Cammie raised her chin. "I know how you feel, Curt, but I haven't been with a man in nearly a year, and right now I don't care about love." She glanced at his strained zipper. "You need this as badly as I do."

"A certain part of me does." With a humorless smile he thrust the robe into her arms. "I know you, Cammie. In the morning, you'll care. I don't think I could handle you hating me or yourself." He set is jaw. "Our friendship is too important to risk for sex."

Darn him, he was right.

He tugged on his shirt. Dazed and shocked at herself but not sorry for what she and Curt had shared, Cammie shrugged into her robe. The soft terry was almost painful against her aroused nipples.

"We didn't used to feel this way about each other," she said, pulling the sash tight and knotting it. "What's happening to us, Curt?"

"We've changed." His dark eyes searched hers. "I want you, Cammie. All the time. And that's just plain wrong."

Knowing he was correct did nothing to douse the fire raging through her. She could think of nothing to say.

"Tonight we stepped over the line. Way over." He

glanced at the half-melted ice packs, scrubbed his hand over his face, and released a weighty breath. Desolation sharpened his features. "Much as it hurts to admit this, I don't think we can be friends anymore."

Sad but true. Cammie gave a mournful nod. "We still have to work together through the wedding." Which wasn't for another two and a half weeks. "There's a second dinner party Friday night, and a bridal shower Saturday afternoon, and Weston expects us both. How do you want to handle that?"

"Go back to the way things were. You stop talking to me, and I'll leave you alone."

The very thought bothered her. "Don't you remember? If we're not friendly to each other, Weston will skewer us. Besides," she said, slipping her hands into her pockets, "I don't want to go back to ignoring you. Why can't we be friends in a professional sense?"

"We tried that at the eighth-grade party, and look where it got us." He shot a hot look at her mouth.

With that one glance, her body began to thrum and ache. Ignoring her feelings, she pressed her point. "We know better now. We're adults and also professionals, and I know we can have a friendly but business-only relationship if we try."

"Business only," Curt repeated. A moment later he gave a reluctant nod. "All right."

"Great," she said. "Let's shake on it." She held out her hand.

His shook his head. "No touching. Not even a handshake. I'll let myself out. Good night, Cammie."

He left without a backward glance.

SITTING IN THE ONLY FAST-FOOD restaurant in town, Curt and his brothers wolfed down their double cheeseburgers and fries. Half a dozen families, most with noisy little kids, sat scattered through the bright room. Back in high school, when Curt's mom had been sick, the Blanco brothers had eaten here often. Not much anymore, but Kit, who liked having them all over for dinner, was working another double shift at the library and they needed food before their Thursday-night volleyball games.

"My team plays the Aces in the field next to Town Hall," Eric said. "What about you guys?"

Curt wiped his mouth with his napkin. "Baseball field, against the High Fives."

"We're at the soccer field with the Top Dawgs," Steven said. "Where you and Cammie knocked heads." His mouth quirked. "Now there's something I wish I'd seen."

Both brothers eyed Curt and he knew they expected him to crack a joke. But he was in no mood for that. "It wasn't funny."

Neither was what had happened later that night. He scowled.

Taken aback, Steven held up his hands, palms out. "Hey, I was only kidding. You and Cammie both are stubborn and hardheaded. You gotta see the humor there…."

At Curt's glare, he shut his mouth.

His brothers exchanged guarded glances. "You're in a fine mood," Eric said. "It was an accident, Curt. Everybody knows that. And you're both okay."

Curt's mouth was full, and he took his time chewing. Since what had happened afterward was no accident, he didn't feel okay. From the moment Cammie had opened the door in her robe and socks, he'd wanted her. Hell, he'd wanted her far longer than that. Try seventeen years.

Two days had passed, and he still got hard just thinking about that. His body had gotten the best of him and he was ticked about his lapse of control. He wasn't sorry, though. Which was why he and Cammie couldn't be friends. They'd only end up doing more of the same—a lot more. Then he'd break her heart. She deserved better.

"I still feel like a jerk," he said.

Both brothers acknowledged the comment with sober faces. "Have you talked to her, to see how she's doing?" Eric asked.

"Nope."

Steven wadded his napkin into a ball. "Think she'll play tonight?"

"Beats me." Curt drained the last of his pop. He hoped she stayed home. He was in no mood to face her, not yet.

Now his brothers looked curious.

"Something we should know?" Steven asked.

Curt shook his head. "What's going on with you and Jules?" he asked Steven.

"Unlike you, I'm not afraid of my feelings. I'm openly nuts about her."

"Afraid?" Curt snorted. "I'm not afraid of anything." Except hurting Cammie. "I don't have feelings for Cammie."

Eric looked skeptical. "You're friends again, right? That counts as feelings."

"I don't want to talk about that." Tired of the conversation, Curt glanced at his watch. "If we want to get to our games on time, we'd best leave now."

As CAMMIE STRAIGHTENED her hair Friday morning, she frowned at her reflection in the bathroom mirror. Her forehead was tender, and no amount of makeup could hide the swollen, purple bump on her forehead. She was too sore to wear makeup, anyway.

She looked like a walking disaster. Grimacing, she unplugged the straightener. With the festivities for Kelly and Rick in full swing, including parties tonight and to-morrow, the timing couldn't have been worse. Then again, by now everyone knew about the accident.

And she was far too busy to waste time worrying about a bruise. For days she'd worked nonstop on last-minute details for tonight's dinner party and tomorrow's bridal shower, the days so full she barely had time to eat.

Let alone think about Curt Blanco.

So what if he kissed like a dream and had the most skilled, clever hands ever? They were wrong for each other. They were hardly even friends, and just when she was getting used to the idea again.

With a wistful sigh she headed for her office. Her parents had called while she was in the shower, but she hadn't heard the phone. They sounded relaxed and happy, and said they'd try to call later. A lot later she hoped, after she pulled herself out of the doldrums.

She sat down at her desk and woke up the computer. Her life was a mess, a worry her parents didn't need, and right now she wasn't sure she could fool them with feigned brightness. For some reason, as Kelly's wed-ding date drew closer, Cammie grew more anxious to find a man for herself.

Who knew why. The location? The one-year anniversary of her breakup with Todd? Which happened to be next week.

They were silly reasons for the desperation grabbing her. Sooner or later she would meet her Mr. Right. In the meantime, there were more pressing problems.

Weston was driving her out of her mind. With the wedding two weeks from tomorrow and parties tonight and tomorrow, he called several times a day. Adding details, changing details, reminding her to do things she'd already taken care of. Aargh!

She called up the Atwood-Mathers Wedding folder where she stored the details for each event on a separate spreadsheet. She brought up the spreadsheet for tonight's dinner and dance on the *Honey Blonde*, the luxurious yacht Weston had rented, and highlighted the to do list. Not that she needed to look at it. The man called so often to add to or change his long list of requirements for the evening, she'd practically memorized it.

He grew more domineering by the day, nitpicking at Cammie's plans and all but plowing over Kelly's wants in favor of his own. His daughter was anxious and unhappy, and he didn't seem to notice or care. Cammie hoped they'd smooth over the bumps in time for Kelly's wedding day to be a joyous one.

She clicked the mouse. Contact the band and make sure they—

The doorbell rang, startling her. Who could that be? Probably the delivery truck with some of the things she'd ordered for tomorrow's bridal shower. Cammie stood. She'd been sitting awhile now, and as she headed for the front door, she massaged the kinks out of her lower back.

To her surprise, Jules stood at the door. Birds chirped and the sun was shining. The late-May air smelled of the sea and the heady sweetness of lilacs from a nearby bush. Cammie had been too busy to even notice until now. She eyed Jules curiously. "What are you doing here?"

"I was in the neighborhood. Why weren't you at volleyball last night?"

"My head, and I'm really under the wire on Kelly's wedding."

Both true, but not the real reason she'd stayed home. She wasn't quite ready to face Curt. Tonight, stuck on the yacht with him, would be a real challenge.

Looking squeamish and slightly green, Jules glanced at Cammie's injury. "Looks like it hurts a lot."

"It's better than it was," Cammie said. "What's up?"

"In case you haven't heard, your team won again last night."

"I hadn't, but you could've called and saved yourself the trip." She widened the door and Jules sauntered in. Dressed in jeans and a tight T-shirt, she obviously wasn't coming from work. "Is the factory closed or something?"

"I have so much vacation time saved that I decided to take the day off," Jules cheerfully explained. "Would you mind if I took some of those lilacs home?"

Like Cammie, she adored the heady scent of the flowers. Never mind that lilac underwear had gotten Cammie into bad trouble the other night… Even though the bump on her head had made her forget about feeling and acting sultry and sensuous, she blamed her bra and panties for her wanton behavior. Sort of. The truth was, Curt turned her on. And how.

"I've been meaning to snip some for myself, but I've

been too busy," Cammie said. "I'll cut us both some." Leaving the door open to air out the house, she led Jules into the living room.

"Would you like coffee or tea?"

"No thanks. Before the games last night, Steven had dinner with Curt and Eric," Jules said as she flopped onto a fat green-and-yellow polka-dot armchair. "He says Curt was in a foul mood."

Cammie sat on the plump, red, green and yellow flowered sofa. "Was he?"

If he was suffering anything like her, with good reason. For days her body had felt hot and sensitive. An edgy restlessness she couldn't shake kept her tossing and turning at night, and when she did sleep, she dreamed of sex. With Curt.

Jules's eyebrows raised. "You sure you're feeling okay?"

"Forget about me. I'm worried about you. You *never* take an unscheduled day off. Are you sick or something?"

Jules shook her head. "Just felt like sleeping in. Besides, it's a beautiful day, and once in a while, a girl deserves a day off. I'm on my way to run errands, but I was passing your house, so I thought I'd stop by."

This didn't sound at all like Jules. Cammie peered closely at her friend, noting her sparkling eyes and glowing skin. Suddenly she understood. "Did Steven spend the night?"

Beaming, Jules nodded. "I tried your trick, Cammie. I wore my sexiest bra and panties to volleyball. He couldn't take his eyes off me. And couldn't get me home fast enough after the game. Then…" Features soft and alive, she stared into space, lost in her own private reverie. "It finally happened. Several times. Wearing sexy undies every day is the best trick ever." She grinned. "Taking them off is even better. Making love with a man you love is amazing."

"I'm truly happy for you," Cammie said. And envious. Her thoughts returned to Curt. If he'd just allow himself to fall in love, her life would be wonderful.... The notion thunderstruck her. Was she in love with Curt?

Jules's blissful expression faded. "I figured you'd be thrilled about Steven and me."

"I am," Cammie said, meaning it. "But I'm also envious. Here I'm the one searching for a man to love and settle down with, and you, who never wanted a serious relationship, find it instead."

"Amazing, isn't it? Don't worry, Cammie, someday it'll happen to you, too." Jules offered a smile meant to reassure.

It already had. Curt was the wrong man for her, but she loved him all the same. An unsettling and unwise turn of events, but there it was. She let out a heavy breath.

"That sounds ominous," Jules said. "Here I am, all wrapped up in myself, when you're a wreck. What's on your mind?"

Cammie picked up a throw pillow and hugged it to her chest. "I don't want to put a damper on your happiness."

"Nothing can do that. What's the matter?"

Needing a friendly, trustworthy ear, Cammie told her everything. "I'm in love with Curt," she finished glumly.

"Oh, dear." Jules bit her lip in commiseration. "I suppose an affair is out of the question now."

"It always was," Cammie said. "Even if I wanted a

purely sexual relationship—and that's not me—he won't even consider it."

Jules stared wide-eyed at her. "You discussed the idea with him?"

"Not in those exact words. But he's known me a long time, and he knows what making love means to me."

"Yet the two of you started the dance down that very path."

"That just sort of happened."

"Uh-huh."

Cammie had no clue how to respond to her friend's knowing look. Explain that she'd been about to combust? "Anyway, before things got too far out of control, Curt stopped."

"That's one decent guy," Jules said. "But then, so is Steven." She shook her head in admiration. "Despite their reputations, the Blanco brothers are good men."

"I know."

"Does Curt know how you feel about him?"

Cammie shook her head. "If he did, we'd go right back to avoiding each other. I don't think I could stand that. We both agree that because we're attracted to each other, we can't be close friends the way we used to be. From now on we'll treat each other as friendly business associates, and nothing more. That's the safest way."

"I'm truly sorry," Jules said. "If there's anything I can do…"

"Introduce me to a man who wants what I want."

"We both know the same people, Cammie. Maybe you should think about which man you want and go after him."

There was the problem. Curt was the only man who

interested her. "Lately I've been too busy to think, let alone figure that out." She picked a speck of lint from the throw pillow. "I've handled dozens of weddings without a hitch, yet the closer we get to Rick and Kelly's wedding, the more nervous I am that I won't find my soul mate."

"Relax," Jules said. "Two weeks won't make much difference. If I were you I'd put off the search till I had more time. Meanwhile, keep wearing that sexy underwear. And be careful. You don't want to look too desperate. That scares men away."

"Good advice." The phone rang, but Cammie made no move to answer it. "That's probably Weston. He keeps calling about tonight and tomorrow."

"I don't know how you stand it." Jules glanced at the ceiling and shook her head. "Someone should slip the man a tranquilizer."

"That'd be nice. Thank goodness Kelly's shower tomorrow is for women only." Except for Curt, taking pictures. "He's not involved with the bachelorette party, either." The only event where Cammie was a participant, not the organizer. Not even Curt was allowed at that. "Weston is driving me up the wall," she added. "I only hope I can keep it together until the wedding."

"It'll all be over soon. Then you can focus on finding a man." Jules glanced at her watch. "I'd better let you get back to work."

They both stood and headed for the door. Cammie held up a finger. "Hold on while I grab the shears and cut the lilacs."

Ten minutes later, clutching a glass jar filled with water and stuffed with flowers, Jules headed for her car. Leaving her own bouquet and the shears on the stoop, Cammie followed.

"Call me if you need me," Jules said at the car.

"Thanks. Please don't tell Steven about our conversation."

"I won't. Keep the faith, Cammie. I have a feeling that the man you're looking for is right in front of you. Once the wedding is over, you'll find him."

Chapter Ten

With the late afternoon sun warm on his back and the ocean breeze cool at his face, Curt lugged two loads of camera equipment onto the *Honey Blonde*, the enormous yacht Weston had rented. The guests weren't due for another hour, but Weston wanted him here early. If the tyrant had had his way, Curt would have shown up hours ago, along with the rest of the hirelings.

This was early enough. Curt dreaded being stuck on the boat, which shoved off at six and was scheduled to dock again shortly after midnight. Which might be great for the guests, but seemed an awfully long time to Curt.

Especially with Cammie on board. Though he hadn't seen her since Tuesday, four days was hardly enough to corral his out-of-control lust. She thought they could be "professional acquaintances." Curt snickered. With his randy body and nonstop sexual fantasies? *I don't think so.*

He headed for the main cabin. The luxurious teak and brass, fancy sofas and bamboo dance floor easily could accommodate the thirty guests. Most of them were from out of town, and if he knew Weston, the powerful man meant to wow them with his wealth. This ought to do the trick. Curt whistled, then dropped his gear in the corner between the bar and the stage, where the six-member jazz band and their technician were setting up.

"About time, Blanco," Weston said in his usual terse voice. "I want photos of people's faces as they walk onto the yacht, so you'd better set up."

"I'm sure they'll be impressed," Curt said.

"I want it on film."

"And you'll get it. Before I set up I want to look around and scope out the best sites for other pictures." And find Cammie. He wanted to get what would be an awkward moment out of the way.

"Make it fast." Weston hurried off, no doubt to needle some other employee.

Curt set off to explore. He strolled past the glassed-in captain's area, where the captain was busy with his own chores, and a head, which was boat lingo for *bathroom*. He peeked through the swinging doors of the big, state-of-the-art galley, where Cammie might be. A lanky, white-coated chef in a tall white hat stood directing four tuxedoed waiters as they loaded trays with hors d'oeuvres. But there was no sign of Cammie.

Disappointed and also relieved, Curt strode to the back of the yacht. Two staterooms and one public head later, he had yet to find her. He climbed down a wide, teak ladder for the lower deck.

He found Rick and Kelly sitting on a plaid sofa in a denlike room with a bar and television. Neither looked happy. Curt figured Weston had something to do with the glum faces. "Hey," he said.

They started, as if they'd been caught doing something clandestine.

"Didn't mean to startle you," he said. "Everything okay?"

"We needed a few minutes alone," Rick said.

Kelly nodded, then lowered her voice. "We're hiding from Daddy. He's a terror tonight."

"So I noticed." Curt gestured at the comfortable, roomy cabin. "Some boat, huh? This thing is as big as all the Blanco houses combined."

"Big or not, Rick can't handle the rocking. He's seasick."

He did look slightly green. "You need fresh air," Curt said.

Rick grimaced and Kelly shook her head. "Daddy's up there, remember?"

"Does he know about this?" Curt asked.

"We both told him, several times, but you know Daddy. He wanted this party on a boat." Kelly shot a fond but worried look at Rick. "Why isn't the motion-sickness drug working?"

"It takes a while," Rick said.

"Maybe you should take another pill."

"Okay."

She kissed his cheek, then jumped up and moved to the wet bar. "I'll be back with some water."

A glance at his watch told Curt time was short. "Gotta run. Hang in there," he said, clapping a hand on Rick's shoulder.

He quickly searched the rest of the lower deck, including two more staterooms. If Cammie was on board, she wasn't down here.

Taking the steps two at a time, he returned to the main deck. Striding forward, he rounded a corner and nearly smashed into her.

"Oops," she said, darting back. "Here we go again."

Curt caught a whiff of lily of the valley and everything flooded back—the feel and taste of her in his arms, her eager response to his touch... Shoving his hands into his trouser pockets he gave a brusque nod. "Sorry about that."

Dressed in low heels and a conservative green dress that hit just above the knee, she looked tame and modest. Underneath she was probably wearing a skimpy little bra and panties that barely covered her. Which color he wondered.

Body stirring to life, he frowned. "I've been searching for you. How's the forehead?"

"Better than it looks." She glanced at his lower face. "What about your jaw?"

"Almost good as new. You missed a great game last night."

"I, um, had to work," she said without meeting his eye. "And anyway, the team seems to be doing fine without me."

Maybe, but Curt didn't find volleyball nearly as enjoyable without her. Safer, though.

As a "professional acquaintance," he could think of nothing more to say. He scratched the back of his neck, his mind a blank.

Looking equally ill at ease, Cammie peered around him. "Have you seen Kelly?"

"Downstairs." Curt shook his head. "Poor Rick is

seasick. They're waiting for his meds to take effect." He lowered his voice. "And hiding out from Weston."

As if Weston heard, his voice roared toward them. "Cammie, get your butt into the galley now!" he bellowed.

She winced. "The master calleth."

Curt stiffened, hating the way his boss treated her. He wasn't sure he could stand six hours of this, and told Cammie so.

"For Kelly's sake and your own job security, let it go. Please."

No man could ignore the plea in her eyes. She was right, too. He couldn't jeopardize his income, not with his father's medical problems. He gave a reluctant nod. "Okay, but I don't like it."

"Thank you," she said with a sigh of relief. "I'd better go now."

She hurried off. Intent on steering as clear of Weston as possible, Curt headed for the main cabin. He'd do the same with Cammie. If he could get through the evening without seeing either of them, tonight wouldn't be half-bad.

HOURS LATER, DRINKS AND DINNER successfully completed and the guests dancing or relaxing at tables around the dance floor, Cammie took a much-needed break from the noise and Weston. His micromanaging was driving her crazy. With dinner over he wasn't likely to come into the galley. She slipped through the swinging doors. The staff had cleaned up and were relaxing in the den on the lower deck, so she had the room to herself.

Famished, she fixed herself a plate of leftovers—Kobe beef, green beans amandine, garlic mashed potatoes and Caesar salad. She plunked onto one of the two stools at the small eating bar, and with a sigh of relief slipped off her shoes.

Thanks to the thick doors, the loud music and conversation outside were pleasantly muted, the perfect background for dinner. She was nearly finished when the doors opened. Noise spilled inside, and Curt strolled in. Seeing her, he hesitated, his pained expression telling her he'd meant to avoid her. The same as she was avoiding him.

Too late for that now. Besides, who said professional acquaintances couldn't share dinner?

"There are leftovers in the fridge," she said. "And bottled water. Help yourself."

He filled a plate, grabbed a bottle and sat down on the stool beside her.

For a short while, neither of them spoke, Cammie picking at the remains of her beef and Curt wolfing down his meal.

"Great food," he said enthusiastically.

Cammie agreed. "We're lucky the caterers were able to make the last-minute changes Weston demanded."

"No luck involved, Cam," Curt said. "Weston owes tonight's success to you."

Cammie dipped her head modestly, but couldn't stop a smile of agreement. "It *is* a good party. Everyone seems to be having fun."

"Except the guests of honor. Did you see Kelly and Rick at dinner? They looked miserable, and I don't think from seasickness."

Cammie sighed. "Why can't Weston leave them alone? Why can't he leave *me* alone?" To her astonishment, angry tears filled her eyes.

"Whoa." Curt set down his fork. He reached out as if to touch her, but instead clenched his hands into fists on the stainless-steel bar. "What'd the bastard do now?"

He was already fed up with Weston. No need to make matters worse. Cammie blinked back the tears. "I'm just tired."

"Tired or not, you don't deserve his crap."

"Only two more weeks, then I'll be free of him. For good. I don't think I'll ever do another party for Weston Atwood. If I change my mind, will you please slap some sense into me?"

"I'd never slap you, but I will shake a finger in your face. Like this." Looking as if he'd sucked a lemon, he wagged his index finger at her.

She laughed.

Curt grinned. "There's that sunshine smile I love."

This was the Curt she used to know, back when they'd been close, platonic friends. Sitting here, talking felt almost like old times.

Cammie savored the moment. "You know about Steven and Jules, right?"

"They're still seeing each other," Curt said. He took a healthy swig of his water. "What's to know?"

She raised her eyebrows and lowered her voice. "He spent the night at her house last night."

"No kidding." Curt chuckled and shook his head. "About time. Steven wasn't the only one who went home with somebody." He returned to his dinner.

Jules hadn't mentioned this. "Don't keep me in suspense," Cammie pressed. "Who else?"

She waited impatiently while Curt finished his mouthful, then wiped his lips. "Billy and Janey Jones."

"Get out!" Cammie smacked his biceps the way she used to. "Did Marcy throw a fit?"

The laughter in Curt's eyes told her he was enjoying this as much as she was. "Apparently it was her idea. She wanted Janey to enjoy Billy as she had, and he was all for it."

"No." Cammie shook her head in wonder. Fiddling with her linen napkin, she sighed. "Sometimes I wish I were like that, able to have a casual affair and move on."

Realizing what she'd just said, she clamped her mouth shut.

Too late. Curt glanced at her mouth, swallowed and raised his gaze to hers. "If you were into short-term relationships, we'd be involved in one right now."

The desire darkening his face and the very thought of having sex with him caused havoc inside her body. Warmth rushed through her and every nerve stood on alert. Afraid of what Curt might see in her eyes, she looked down at her lap. Her legs were crossed at the knee, and her skirt was halfway up her thigh. A tiny run in her hose had started someplace higher up and was almost to her knee. Frowning, she tugged the hemline, but the run was still visible.

Curt cleared his throat. "You have a run in those stockings."

"I just realized that. You wouldn't happen to have a bottle of nail polish in your pocket? To stop it from getting worse."

"Afraid not."

"And I didn't bring a spare pair." Cammie frowned. "I don't want to look tacky. Now what am I supposed to do?"

"Take them off," he suggested. Though his voice held

not a trace of sexual innuendo, his warm, focused expression was pure need.

Cammie's pulse rate sped up. "Bare legs at a formal party?" she said, to her own ears sounding coolly unaffected.

"People are boozed up and dancing, or looking at the moon and the stars," Curt said. "Nobody'll know except you and me."

"I doubt I'll have time to take them off. The minute I leave this galley, Weston will be on my case."

"Then do it now. I'll stand guard and make sure no one gets in."

She searched his face carefully before nodding. "All right, but turn your back."

The instant Curt pivoted toward the double doors, Cammie reached under her skirt and pulled the elastic over her hips.

"You wearing lilac underwear again?" he said in a strained voice.

"Curt!" she said, her face warming. She whisked off the hose, then smoothed her dress. "That is none of your business."

"Can't fault a man for asking. What color are they?"

Bronze satin, but he'd never know. "Maybe I'm wearing an old cotton set. You can turn around now," she said as she lobbed the damaged hose into the trash.

He spun toward her, his eyes hot as they skimmed her body. "Cotton or silk, in my book you're a ten."

Her body stretched toward him of its own volition, and a wicked idea crossed her mind—to show him the bronze panties. All she needed to do was lift her skirt....

Appalled at herself, she turned to search for her shoes, which she'd left by her stool.

"Best get back to my camera," Curt said in a gruff voice.

He wheeled away. Then he was gone.

With shaking hands, Cammie loaded the dishwasher. Time spent with Curt was dangerous. To avoid him she could drop out of volleyball, but she couldn't back out of Kelly's wedding.

Two more weeks, and she wouldn't have to see him except now and then, when they ran into each other. Meanwhile, she would pull herself together. She would make herself stop wanting him. She would!

Somehow.

Chapter Eleven

While twenty jabbering women of all ages sat crowded around Kelly, Curt stood at the back of the Matherses', Rick's parents, small living room. He never had photographed an all-female bridal shower before. He was the only male present and felt like a stranger in a strange land.

At the moment the women were absorbed by Kelly and the fruit-and-cheese plate and desserts Cammie was passing around, and paid no attention to him. With Weston banned from the party, everyone was in good spirits, especially Cammie and Kelly.

As both guest and organizer, Cammie seemed far more relaxed than last night. Except when she glanced at or spoke to him. Then she wouldn't meet his eye. Curt was equally uncomfortable, and his semiarousal was starting to feel like a permanent state. Her short red dress didn't help matters. Was she wearing the red bra and panties? At that intriguing image, his body tightened. Willing a certain part of his anatomy to behave—not likely—he zoomed in on Kelly.

Today she was animated and happy, the way brides should be. Mrs. Mathers looked pleased, too. Curt had taken dozens of photos of her and Rick's dad on the yacht last night. She seemed to like her future daughter-in-law and vice versa, which was good. Cynic that he was, Curt wondered how she'd feel when Kelly and Rick separated and divorced someday.

Suddenly Cammie clinked a spoon against her punch cup to catch everyone's attention. The room quieted.

"Before Kelly opens her gifts, we're going to play a game," she announced. She passed out pencils and sheets of paper. "This is a memory game. The winner gets a prize, so no comparing notes." Her gaze settled on him. "Curt, may I see you in the kitchen?"

"Me?" he asked, garnering laughter. "What for?"

"This won't take long and it won't hurt. You'll get back to your camera in time to snap plenty of pictures." Cammie headed for the kitchen as if she expected him to follow.

The last thing he wanted was to participate in a silly game. He was here to work, period. But with every female staring at him, he was stuck. Reluctantly he followed Cammie into the kitchen. She shut the door.

"What do I have to do?" he asked.

"Nothing too taxing," she said, her eyes twinkling. "Just carry this tray into the living room, walk slowly around the room so everyone can see the contents, and come back into the kitchen. Then stay out of sight until everyone records what they remember."

That sounded easy enough. "Anybody could do this," he said. "Why me?"

"Because you're the only man." Cammie smiled. "It was Kelly's idea."

"I was hired to take photos, not parade around the room."

"Don't be a spoilsport, Curt. With Weston controlling everything else, let's give Kelly this one small thing."

Damn but she was cute when she scolded him. "All right," he said.

"Thank you." Cammie handed him a sliver tray containing kitchen gadgets, spices, a white satin garter and a framed photo of Kelly and Rick. She gestured Curt out.

Feeling acutely awkward, he made his way through the room—given the crowd, no easy feat—with the tray. A few minutes later, he returned to the kitchen.

"Now, stay here," Cammie said. "I'll let you know when to come back out."

The house was small and her voice carried easily as she explained the game to the guests. "You think you're supposed to write down what's on the tray, right? Sorry ladies, what I want to know is, what is Curt wearing? Write it down and remember, there are prizes. So don't share information."

Laughter erupted, followed by silence. Curt figured they were writing away.

"Come on out, Curt," Cammie called a while later.

Hating the way they looked him over, he stood in the living room in his black slacks, blue dress shirt, tie and wingtips until the winner was announced. Kelly's aunt Ida won a gift certificate to Cranberries-to-Go, a local tourist shop.

"Thanks, Curt." Cammie clapped, and the other women joined in.

Curt shrugged. He grabbed his camera and did his best to blend in with the woodwork.

Not so difficult, with Kelly about to open her gifts. Besides the usual household stuff, there were more personal things—a sexy nightgown and a box of massage oils.

Curt imagined Cammie in the slinky black nightgown. He'd peel it off, then rub massage oil over her back and hips, and maybe her breasts. He swallowed hard.

As if she felt his hungry stare, she caught his gaze. The heat in her face only fueled his need. Damn. Pretending he needed to change the film, he turned his back on those eyes. And prayed for four o'clock, when he could get out of there.

CURT WAS PACKING UP TO LEAVE when Cammie pulled him aside. "Could I talk to you?" she said in a low voice. "Privately?"

Ignoring the raised eyebrows of the other women, Curt followed her into the small den off the living room. She closed the door, a risky move given the state of his body. Wary, he moved behind the Barcalounger.

"What?" he asked, brusque and unhappy.

Cammie looked equally wretched. "This friendly professional thing isn't working."

"Tell me about it." He scrubbed his hand over his face. "Short of quitting, which isn't an option, there's not much we can do but steer clear of each other as much as possible over the next two weeks."

"I'm not so sure." She fidgeted with her hair, then looked him straight in the eye. "Maybe we should just make love and get it over with."

Words he'd never expected to hear. His jaw dropped. "Are you nuts?"

"I'm perfectly sane, and I've been thinking about it a lot." Her jaw set in determination. "I want to."

How could she sit there and propose something so dangerous without considering the consequences? As badly as Curt wanted to take her up on the offer, he wasn't about to risk hurting her. He shook his head. "Not with me, you don't. What you want is to meet a nice guy and settle down for life."

"That's right."

Totally confused, he frowned. "We both know I'm not that kind of guy."

"Right again. Hear me out," she said. "Jules says men can sense when a woman is desperate. Maybe that's why I haven't had a date in a while." She caught her lip between her teeth and dropped her gaze to the blue carpet. "I'm thinking that maybe if you and I have sex, I'll calm down."

She'd astonished him yet again. He massaged the back of his neck and lifted the corner of his mouth. "You sound like a guy, trying to get up a woman's skirt."

She didn't so much as crack a smile, just kept gnawing on her poor lip. "It's not funny."

"That's something we agree on." Nothing remotely funny about the desire burning in him or her dangerous proposal. No matter what she believed, if they made love she was bound to get hurt. She was made that way. Refusing to cause her more pain, he shook his head. "This is a very bad idea."

"Please, Curt, I need you." Her eyes held a hint of desperation.

That plea was hard to resist. To keep from racing toward her and pulling her close, he gripped the Barcalounger. "Cammie, I—"

"You should see my underwear today," she interrupted with a shaky smile.

She had him there. Imagination on full tilt, he glanced at her breasts, then at her hips. Suddenly he was hard with need. He cleared his throat. "The red ones?"

"Take me to bed and find out." Again with the lip.

It took every ounce of willpower he possessed to stay where he was. "Let me think about it," he ground out.

She nodded. "I'll be at home tonight, and I'll be waiting."

Cammie opened the door. She left. Curt sucked in a breath and attempted to think straight. Even with lust clouding his judgment, he knew he couldn't give in. And that was that. Mind made up and groin back to normal, he strode into the living room to tell her.

But she was surrounded by chattering women, and he was in no mood for small talk. Curt decided to let her know later. He packed his equipment, said his goodbyes and left.

RIGHT AFTER DINNER THAT SAME day, Curt stood at Cammie's door, his jaw set with grim determination. This time of year, the days were long. Tonight though, heavy rain clouds darkened the sky, a fitting tribute to his rotten mood.

Three long, miserable hours had passed since she'd invited him to make love with her, hours spent tamping down his raging need and fighting to stay rational. His decision stood, and he was here to turn her down. Rather than ring the bell, he knocked twice, sharp raps that stung his knuckles. Then he shoved his hand into the hip pocket of his jeans.

His fingers connected with several foil packets. Why he'd brought condoms along was anybody's guess. Glaring at a robin pulling worms, he crossed his arms instead.

Cammie opened the door.

While he stood there, shifting and as nervous as hell, she smiled. "I was hoping it was you. Please come in."

He'd explain again why they never would have sex, then leave. Grim-faced, Curt moved past her. Since he wasn't staying, he stayed in the entry. A fat vase of lilacs sat in the recessed shelf on one side, the smell filling his senses. "Those flowers smell good," he commented.

"Thanks." Cammie shut the door. "They're from the bush out front." A saucy tilt to her head, she leaned against the door.

She was barefoot and wearing a baggy T-shirt and loose calf-length pants, a welcome respite from the short skirts she usually wore.

All the same, she looked hot. She could have been in chain mail and he'd still want her. As for the scarlet nail polish on her toes... Curt gritted his teeth against the need to pull her close, kiss her and more. "I'm here to talk," he said.

"Oh." She sighed with obvious disappointment and pushed away from the door. "Then you may as well come into the living room."

His eyes settled on her luscious behind. Of course with the baggy T-shirt he couldn't see much, but his imagination filled in what was hidden. Hardly aware of himself, he groaned.

Cammie sat down on one side of the sofa, leaving plenty of space for him. "What's wrong?"

"What isn't?" Ignoring the sofa, he sank heavily onto the rocking chair.

"If you don't want to have sex with me, that's okay," she said, but her eyes were dark with pain.

Great, he'd hurt her already. "Believe me, I want to." He looked into her gaze, letting her see the desire in his eyes. "You don't know how badly."

The hurt expression changed to confusion. "But?"

"What if this whole thing backfires, and you fall for me?" At the heavy thought, he gave his head a dire shake.

"I'm a big girl, Curt."

"With sensitive feelings. A few seconds ago, when you assumed I didn't want to make love with you... I saw the wounded look on your face. Hurting you is not something I want on my conscience."

"But you're hurting me now, Curt. All I think about is us together. If we don't make love, I'll keep fantasizing about you. How will I ever meet other eligible men?"

Her dead-serious expression almost convinced him of her twisted logic. "That's ridiculous," he said, his control slipping.

"Is it? Don't you want to get rid of that longing, too?"

Her big doe eyes probed his, and for an instant he lost himself in their silver-blue depths. "Yeah," he admitted.

"Since we both want each other, what's stopping us?"

Her words and the raw desire in her eyes snapped the last of his self-control. "You win. Let's make love—if you're sure," he added, to give her an out.

"I'm sure."

With that he stood, moved to the sofa and pulled her to her feet.

CAMMIE HEADED FOR THE BEDROOM on trembling legs, the only sounds her pounding heart and the thud of Curt's footsteps beside her. He said nothing and neither did she. She couldn't have spoken now if she wanted to. For all her talk, she was scared.

Silly. She wanted this more than she'd ever wanted anything.

Curt didn't mean to hurt her, but she already loved him. Things couldn't be any worse than that. At least now she'd have this one night to remember. Then she could move on.

Because she'd expected this to happen, she'd showered with her scented lily-of-the-valley bath gel. She'd changed the sheets and turned down the bed. A second vase of lilacs on the dresser filled the room with the same heady scent as the entry.

Preferring the waning daylight to the artificial light of the bedside table lamp, Cammie slanted the blinds and left off the lights. She stood beside the shuttered window and turned wordlessly to Curt.

His face darkened with yearning as he strode toward her. Pulling her into his arms, he kissed her. Slowly and gently, until heat rippled through Cammie and she forgot her fears. Wrapping her arms around his neck, she pushed closer. His body was hard. *Everywhere.* For her.

Moments later Curt broke the kiss. "Let's get rid of some of these clothes," he said, as breathless as if he'd just run a race.

Watching each other, they removed their shirts.

His heavy-lidded eyes smoldered. "The red set. I hoped so."

"It matches my nail polish," Cammie said.

"Nice touch. Now let me see those panties. Take off your pants."

Feeling deliciously uninhibited, she smiled. "I will, if you will."

"One minute." Curt reached into his back pocket. He pulled out a handful of condoms and tossed them onto the bedside table.

"And here I thought I talked you into having sex tonight."

He gave her a sheepish look. "I'm always prepared. A hold over from my Boy Scout days."

"You don't need those, Curt. I'm on the pill and I'm clean."

"Me, too. Now that that's settled..." He nodded at her cargo pants.

Holding his gaze, Cammie shimmied out of them. His face taut with desire, he quickly shoved off his jeans. He wore burgundy boxers, and he was gloriously erect.

Her heart thudded. She hadn't been with a man in so long. "Burgundy clashes with red," she said.

"Then we'd best get naked."

Within moments her bra and panties lay beside his boxers on the carpet.

Curt stared at her, his throat working as if he found swallowing difficult. "You are so beautiful. More beautiful than I ever imagined."

"You've imagined me naked?"

He nodded. "Since we were fourteen. That's how long I've wanted you."

"Wow," Cammie said. "I never guessed." If only

wanting was the same as love. Though right now, she didn't care about anything except joining her body with his. "I hope I don't disappoint you."

"Are you kidding? Already this is better than any fantasy." Curt's reassuring tone and awed expression steadied her nerves and bolstered her confidence.

"Well, now you can have me. In the flesh." She walked into his arms.

He held her reverently, the proof of his need hard against her belly. Tenderness swelled her heart, and she was so overcome with feeling that tears gathered in her eyes. Hastily she willed them away. If Curt noticed, he might stop.

He led her to the bed, cupped her shoulders and pushed her lightly onto the mattress, so that she was sitting with her feet on the floor. Kneeling between her thighs, he wrapped his arms around her waist and rested his head against her rapidly thudding heart.

His soft hair teased her breasts, and his warm breath whispered tantalizingly across her stomach. He kissed her navel once, then pulled away to reach for the bed pillows and bunch them behind her. "Lie back," he said.

He fondled and licked her breasts, making her writhe with pleasure. Then, taking his slow, sweet time, he kissed his way down her rib cage, to her navel, and…

"Sweet heaven," Cammie moaned as his hot breath touched her aching center.

Then he was tasting her, his clever tongue moving her closer and closer to climax. Aching and desperate, she lifted her hips.

Curt inserted two fingers inside and continued to tongue her. Any second now… "Stop." With effort she pushed him away. "I don't want to climax alone. Come up here beside me."

"Exactly what do you have in mind?" With a sexy smile, his eyes darkening with hunger, he joined her on the bed.

"You'll find out." Mimicking his actions, she nuzzled his nipples, licked his navel and moved lower. Curt hissed in a breath. She licked his hard length, then closed her mouth over the head of his shaft. Groaning, he pushed upward. That she could pleasure him this way made her feel powerful, sexy and potent.

Moments later he gasped, stopping her. "No more."

Suddenly she was on her back with Curt poised over her, his face more open with feeling than she'd ever seen. Heat glittered in his eyes. "Ready?"

In answer, Cammie wrapped her legs around his hips. He entered her, pushing deep.

She moaned. Immediately Curt froze. "Am I hurting you?"

"No. I like it. A lot." She kissed him.

"You feel so damn good," he whispered against her mouth.

"I know." She could barely focus on the words. Her whole world was Curt and the two of them, joined as one. She gripped his back. "Please, Curt, I need you now. Hard and fast."

"Hard." He thrust into her. "And fast," he grunted, moving in and out.

The bedroom faded and she lost herself. Her climax shattered her world. Curt let go at the same time, and she swore the very earth convulsed.

When it was over he kissed her lips, then rolled off

her. Spent and fulfilled, Cammie snuggled against his side. "That was wonderful."

"The best." He rubbed the underside of his chin over the top of her head.

"We're good together, aren't we?"

"Better than good. Red-hot."

Though she couldn't see Curt's face, she heard the satisfaction in his voice.

Propping herself on her elbow, she noted the relaxed, satisfied grin on his face. Arching her brows, she smiled into his eyes. "Want to spend the night and do this some more?"

"Now there's a tough offer to refuse," he said. An instant later his grin faltered. "You're not falling for me, are you?"

"Of course not," she lied. *I already have.* Sex had only deepened her feelings.

"Good," Curt said, but he looked doubtful. Untangling his arms and legs, he scooted away. "I'll get you a towel. Be right back."

She watched him pad to the bathroom. He was tall, muscled and lean, magnificent. And she loved him, so much, her heart hurt.

Thank goodness he'd never know.

CLEANING UP IN THE BATHROOM, Curt cursed himself a thousand ways to Sunday. Cammie was passionate and eager and willing. The sex had been dynamite, the best ever. But this whole thing was one huge mistake. If he'd been thinking with his brain instead of another part of his body, he'd have done the right thing, turned her down and left.

He splashed water on his face, noting the love bite

on his neck. How could a man focus on doing the right thing when a woman like Cammie wanted him?

Spending the night seemed like a great idea. Until she'd looked at him with that soft, tender expression. She didn't have to say a word—her face said everything.

She was in love with him. He'd been right all along. She wasn't a casual-sex kind of woman.

The last thing he wanted was to hurt her. But he was incapable of loving her or anyone else, and he couldn't make the commitment she so badly wanted and deserved.

Remorse washed over him, along with self-contempt. He scrubbed his hand over his face and cursed again.

What had he done?

Chapter Twelve

One look at Curt's closed expression and tense jaw, and Cammie knew he wouldn't be staying.

What had changed?

She wanted to ask but was afraid of what he might say. Mustering a cheerful smile, she caught the towel he tossed her. "I changed my mind." She sat up and leaned against the headboard, tucking the covers under her arms. "I don't think you should spend the night."

"Wasn't planning on it." He stepped into his boxers, then his jeans. Last, he pulled his shirt over his head.

"Are you upset about something?" she asked.

"As a matter of fact, I am." Sitting on the floor, Curt pulled on his socks. He shoved his feet into his sneakers and quickly tied the laces.

When he said nothing more, she frowned. "Are you going to tell me, or would you rather I guess?"

"You already know the answer, Cammie." Eyes blazing, he pushed to his feet. "You're in love with me."

She should have been embarrassed, but his tight-lipped disapproval infuriated her. "Of all the pompous, conceited things to say." Holding onto the sheet, she scrambled from bed. As she wrapped it securely around her, she glared at Curt. "I am not in love with you."

"Oh, yes you are. Dammit, Cammie." Hands low on his hips, eyes dark and narrowed, he looked fierce and angry. "We both know I can't love you back." He shook his head. "I knew we shouldn't have made love."

Crossing her arms, she eyed him. "You said you enjoyed it."

"I did," he said, his face softening a fraction. An instant later he set his jaw. "That doesn't mean it should have happened." He retrieved her bra and panties and set them on the dresser, beside the lilacs. "I don't want to be one more guy who broke your heart."

"I never expected or asked for your love. All I wanted was for you to make love with me. You did, and it made me very happy. So you can forget about my heart. I certainly have." She pivoted away and marched into the bathroom. Snatching her robe from the hook on the door, she slipped into it. She stuffed the sheet, which smelled of her and Curt and sex into the laundry hamper.

When she came out Curt was about to strip the rest of the bed. "Just what do you think you're doing?" Cammie said, glaring at him.

"You put one sheet in the laundry. I'm helping you with the rest of—"

"I don't want your help," she said, furious. At him, at herself, at the situation. "Now, why don't I walk you to the door." Before she made things worse and cried.

She stalked down the hall to the front door. Head high, she opened it and ushered him out. "Good night, Curt."

"Night," he said.

She closed and locked the door. Her lovely afterglow was gone, but at least her pride was intact. Her heart, however, was painfully cracked.

She heard Curt's car purr to life. Once she was sure he was gone, the tears came.

DRESSED IN HER BRIDAL GOWN, Kelly stood before the three-way mirror in Mrs. Nevers's shop. "Wow," she said, staring at her reflection. "I look just the way I always dreamed I would."

"You're absolutely gorgeous," Cammie breathed. She loved everything about Kelly's dress—the fitted, white satin bodice; the tiny pearls edging the cap sleeves, square neckline and nipped waist; and the soft, full skirt.

"Thank you." Smiling broadly, Kelly turned slightly, revealing a train and more pearls.

Cammie was beginning to doubt she'd ever be a bride. Her eyes filled. "I think I'm going to cry," she said. Out of happiness for her friend, she sternly told herself, not her own broken dreams.

"Me, too." Mrs. Nevers sniffled. "You look like an angel." She shook her head in admiration. "What a beautiful bride you'll be."

Kelly flushed. She looked so happy, so in love, that it hurt to look at her. Pretending to search out a tissue, Cammie dipped her head.

Stop it, Cammie. If she never found a husband— well, maybe she deserved what she got. Her judgment regarding men always had been shaky, and Saturday night proved that tenfold. Making love with Curt had been a terrible idea. Because instead of getting him out of her system, she loved him more than ever.

And the worst of it was, he'd guessed.

She'd tried her best to hide her feelings, but he knew her too well. How infuriating and embarrassing that was. She never wanted to see or talk to him again. Once the wedding was over, she would do everything possible to avoid him. She'd done it before, with reasonable success. She could do it again.

"Cammie?" Kelly said, looking puzzled. "Are you feeling okay?"

"Terrific." She pasted a happy grin on her face. "You're a true wonder, Mrs. Nevers."

Kelly nodded. "Thank you so much."

"My pleasure, darling." The older woman seemed to grow an inch. She glanced at Cammie. "If you'll unbutton Kelly's dress, dear, I'll go and get your outfit."

As Cammie stepped onto the raised platform to unhook the pearl buttons down the back of the gown, Kelly sighed. A heavy, world-weary sound at odds with the occasion.

"That doesn't sound happy at all," Cammie said.

"You're right." Shooting a furtive look around to make sure Mrs. Nevers wasn't within hearing range, Kelly lowered her voice. "Much as I love this dress, the truth is, I'd rather elope. I'm seriously considering it."

Cammie stopped tinkering with the buttons and gaped at her. "You put that idea right out of your head, Kelly Atwood! Your father would have a heart attack."

"I didn't say I'm going to, I said I'm thinking about it. Don't worry, Rick refuses even to discuss the subject. He says I owe Daddy this wedding."

"I agree," Cammie said. "You're his only child, Kelly, and this is a major milestone in your life. Don't deprive him of sharing it with you."

"I couldn't if I wanted to. Do you know he's been

calling me six and seven times a day? He's driving me out of my mind." She curled her hands into fists and tightened her jaw. "Sometimes I don't think I can stand him another minute."

Cammie shared the sentiment, but she decided not to say so. "Your father is a bundle of nerves," she soothed. "He's been calling me, too." No doubt bugging Curt as well. Not that Cammie knew. She hadn't seen or talked to him since Saturday night. "Hang in there. Only ten more days. Then you'll be free of him. It's going to be a beautiful wedding, a memory you'll cherish forever." She looked into Kelly's face. "Promise me you won't lose sight of that."

"I'll try." A wobbly smile followed. "Will you do something for me, Cammie?"

"Anything."

"Cancel the fireworks."

She'd already paid the deposit for a fifteen-minute display over the ocean. "But your father wants—"

Kelly stamped her foot, causing the platform floor to shake. "For once will you leave him out of this? This is Rick's and my wedding, remember? Yet Daddy gets everything he wants. Can you please just do this one thing *we* want?"

She looked so desperate, Cammie nodded. "All right, but when your father finds out, there'll be hell to pay." Just thinking about his fury made her shudder.

"We won't tell him until after the dress rehearsal. By then it'll be too late to change things."

"I suppose you want me to tell him?" Cammie asked.

Kelly bit her lip, then shook her head. "It's my decision and I'll tell him." But she looked scared half to death.

"We'll do it together," Cammie suggested.

Some of the tension eased from Kelly's shoulders. "Okay. Thanks."

Mrs. Nevers returned with three hangers, which she hung in the dressing room Cammie had used before. "Let's get you out of your dress, Kelly." With deft hands she removed the gown. While she hung it, Kelly dashed into the second dressing room where she'd left her clothes, and pulled the curtain.

"Proper foundations are essential to a smooth, finished look," Mrs. Nevers commented. "I hope you're wearing the appropriate items?"

Proper wasn't the word for her lingerie. Curt would call it *erotic*. For the life of her, Cammie couldn't stem a hot flush. "I don't know, but the color matches."

"Show me." Mrs. Nevers waved her into the fitting room.

"I want to see, too," Kelly said, buttoning her slacks as she joined the dressmaker.

Self-conscious, Cammie pulled her short, electric-blue knit dress over her head.

"Ooh, the rose-color set," Kelly said. "Pretty." She frowned. "I wish you'd take off those panty hose, though, so Mrs. N. could see the heart embroidered on your bikinis."

Curt would love the little embellishment, Cammie thought. But he'd never see it. "These are control tops, a girl's best friend."

"You have a nice figure," Mrs. Nevers said, "but this is a tight skirt, so I agree. Control-top panty hose. Shimmery, with a touch of blush. From what I can see, your panties don't have many seams. That's good." She raised her gaze to Cammie's chest. "That bra is skimpy but gives you decent support." Satisfied, she nodded. "Your underwear is exactly right. Go ahead, put on your blouse, skirt and shoes. Come out when you're ready, and we'll try on the jacket."

"Do you need me to help with anything?" Kelly asked.

Cammie studied the row of silk-covered buttons down the back of her blouse. "Could you help me with these buttons?"

She slipped her arms through the sleeveless, cowl-neck blouse, the soft silk whispering over her skin. Kelly buttoned her into the form-hugging garment and murmured with pleasure. "This is exquisite, Cammie."

Cammie studied herself in the mirror. The deep rose color set off her pale skin, making it seem to glow with life. Glowing, and no one to appreciate it. How pitiful was that?

"This is the second time you've pulled that gloomy face. Sure you're okay?" Kelly asked.

Kelly had enough on her plate. Not wanting to burden her further, Cammie nodded. "I'm fine," she said in a bright voice. "You go on out with Mrs. Nevers. I'll be there shortly."

She pulled on the pencil skirt. A shade darker than the blouse, it fit like a second skin, tight yet flattering. Like its muslin prototype, the hemline stopped a scant inch above the knee, but the five-inch side slits that would make it possible for her to walk revealed plenty of leg. She stepped into the dressy sandals she'd bought last time she and Kelly had been here. Now she looked sophisticated, taller and more slender than she'd ever imagined.

Eager to show Kelly and Mrs. Nevers, and to try on

the matching jacket, she pulled the curtain aside and walked out.

Kelly whistled. "Look out, world."

"Step onto the platform so you can see yourself in the three-way mirror," Mrs. Nevers directed.

Thanks to the slits, Cammie stepped up easily.

"It's a beautiful fit." Mrs. Nevers held out the jacket. "Now try this on."

The fitted garment flared slightly at the hips, reminding Cammie of a budding flower. And the color!

Wait till Curt saw her in this. But his opinion no longer mattered. She pasted a smile on her face. "I really like it."

"Like it? You look amazing," Kelly enthused.

"Some lucky man is going to see you in that outfit and snatch you up," Mrs. Nevers stated with conviction.

They were right. Cammie would move past Curt Blanco, find her soul mate and never look back. She knew it. This time, she smiled for real.

"THANKS FOR THE RIDE," Eric said as Curt drove toward the exit of the high-school parking lot Tuesday night. "Sure you don't mind giving up the chance to drink beer with your buddies?"

Curt shook his head. He was in no mood to socialize.

No game tonight, but his team had practiced against Eric's on the soccer field. Where the whole mess between him and Cammie had started.

If they hadn't collided, he wouldn't have stopped by her house that night. They wouldn't have taken off their shirts and shared those mind-numbing kisses. And he wouldn't have wanted her so badly that he'd come back for more, when he knew what that meant to her.

Which was a total crock, since with or without that accident, he'd wanted her. Always had. Hell, still did.

But he'd never meant to act on his desires. That mistake would not be repeated. Ever. Once the wedding was over he intended to steer clear of Cammie, as much as was possible in Cranberry. And the car in front of him was taking its sweet time pulling out. He leaned on the horn.

Earning a mild frown from Eric. Curt turned and headed down the dual-lane road. Heavy clouds filled the night sky, and beyond the halo of streetlights and the beams of his headlights, the surroundings were dark.

"You think Steven and Jules will stay together?" Eric said after a long silence.

Curt shrugged. "Maybe for a month or two."

"I don't know," Eric said. "I've never seen Steven like this. He's talking forever. I'm beginning to think he means it."

"Like that could happen." A sneer lifted the corner of Curt's mouth. "He's a Blanco, remember?"

"Well, *this* Blanco—" Eric poked his thumb at his own chest "—is happily settled down and not about to change that. Kit's the best thing that's ever happened to me. But you already know that. No reason why Steven can't feel that way about Jules."

As usual, Curt was the only brother who refused to wear blinders. He scoffed. "That'd be the day."

"When you find the right woman, you'll change your tune," Eric said.

He shook his head. "Since I'm not looking, that won't happen."

Cammie was, though. Damning himself again for hurting her, he signaled and moved into the left lane.

Tired of making conversation with Eric and eager to shut off his brain, he turned the radio to the oldies station. A Marvin Gaye song was playing.

Eric sang a few bars, then stopped. "I didn't see Cammie tonight. Hasn't she missed several games? What'd she do, drop out?"

"Her forehead was all bruised up," Curt reminded him. "Today she went to Portland with Kelly, to try on their dresses for the wedding. She's probably not back yet."

He couldn't help wondering which bra and panty set she'd worn for that. No matter which one she chose, she was sure to look hot. Miserable, he cranked up the music.

"So she's not planning to quit?" Eric said over the music.

Ahead, the light turned yellow. Curt slowed and braked to a stop. "Hell if I know."

Even over the music he sounded cranky. This time Eric frowned. "I thought you two talked about stuff now."

Oh, they'd talked, all right. Curt recalled that loaded conversation, the one where Cammie said she wished she could be like Marcy, have a fling and move on. And he'd replied that she wasn't built that way. Why hadn't he remembered his own words?

Feeling lower than low and desperate to turn off his brain, he tapped his fingers impatiently against the steering wheel. "You talk to Pop lately?"

"This afternoon, as a matter of fact. It's not good." Eric looked solemn and worried. "He's deteriorating. Now the doctors are saying if he doesn't have surgery he may never walk again."

Curt swore and turned down the music. "Why didn't somebody tell me?"

"I'm telling you now. Like I said, I only found out a little while ago myself."

"He'll have the surgery, period," Curt said. "Even if we have to carry him there kicking and screaming."

"Now that he knows the alternative, I'm sure we'll be able to talk him into doing the right thing. *If* he's not stressed over how to pay for it."

Curt rolled his eyes. "He knows we're handling the bills. That's why we're all busting our balls working extra jobs."

Eric nodded. "You know Pop. He won't spend the money unless we have every penny in advance."

Given their background, understandable. Bankruptcy did that to a man. Curt glanced at Eric. "We're almost there, right? Once Weston gives me that big fat check he owes me, we'll have enough for the surgery and the physical therapy after. I'll call Pop tonight and remind him of that."

"Good idea," Eric said. "When exactly will you get that big fat check?"

"Right after Kelly and Rick's wedding."

"Then we may as well schedule the surgery." After a beat of silence, Eric frowned at him. "What'd you do to her?"

"Her?" Curt feigned confusion, but he knew exactly who his brother meant. Eric always did have a one-track mind. No way he'd get off the subject until his questions were addressed. The light turned green and he headed forward.

"Don't play games with me, little brother. I know you, and you're acting like a man with a guilty conscience."

Trust Eric to hit the mark. Curt had done the one thing

he never wanted to do—hurt Cammie. Just call him King Screw-up. Wincing, he rolled his shoulders. "I don't want to talk about it." He turned onto Eric's street.

"So don't. But whatever happened, you ought to talk to *her* and straighten things out."

"Since we're not even friends anymore, that's not gonna happen." Stating that aloud felt empty and lonely.

"The friendship thing fizzled? That didn't last long."

Wouldn't you know, "Can't Fight This Feeling," an REO Speedwagon hit from the eighties, came on. Curt turned it off.

"Aah," Eric said, sounding as if he'd discovered electricity.

"What's that supposed to mean?" Curt braked to a stop in front of Eric's bungalow. The porch light was on, and the house looked cozy and welcoming. Kit was inside, waiting for him. Curt had nobody and nothing waiting for him except a cold beer and for one moment he envied his brother. But he wouldn't envy him when the marriage fell apart.

"Cammie means something to you, Curt. She always has. Don't let that slide."

"Too late for that." Curt couldn't hide his anguish.

Eric gave him a shrewd look. "Know what I think? You're in love with her."

Curt snorted. If only that were true. "The hell you say." Anxious to get rid of his brother, he gestured toward the house. "Kit's waiting for you, so go on."

Eric opened his door. "Think about what I said."

"I don't love Cammie," Curt insisted. "I'm not built for love."

Chapter Thirteen

"I can't believe you waited this long to buy Kelly's bachelorette gift," Jules said when Cammie picked her up from work Wednesday afternoon. "The party is only four days from now."

"Hello, I've been swamped," Cammie replied.

And maybe a tad preoccupied, too, dreaming about and wanting Curt. But she was over that now. Over him. With effort she summoned her newfound determination to move beyond Curt Blanco, find another man and never look back.

Straightening her shoulders, she signaled, turned and headed for the Lacy Lady, a new women's boutique downtown. After a long, economic slump, Cranberry was thriving and growing. The successful, upscale boutique was one of several that had recently opened.

"I appreciate your coming with me to find something."

"Are you kidding?" Jules said. "After what Cinnamon told me? Apparently the Lacy Lady recently added a new line of lingerie to their inventory." Jules arched her eyebrows. "Sexy lingerie. Last week her husband, Nick, bought her the most gorgeous satin nightie there."

She grinned. "I could use a slinky new teddy. Steven would love that." Her grin softened and went dreamy. "Correction, he'd love to get me out of it."

Cammie understood perfectly. Curt certainly had appreciated her skimpy underwear, but he'd liked her even better without it. Her body filled with longing and her heart ached. *You're over him*, she sternly reminded herself as she braked for the red light.

"Did I say something I shouldn't have?" Jules asked, tilting her head. "Or maybe you're upset because of the date?"

"What date?"

"A year ago today you called off your wedding."

With all that had happened, Cammie had forgotten. "You're right. Wow." She thought about last year, but felt nothing but a minor twinge of embarrassment. No pain, not over that. "I'm not upset at all," she said. "Kelly and I got back late last night, and I've been up since dawn, working." She'd already told Jules about the fitting, but not about what had happened with Curt. Now *that* hurt, but she felt too raw to share. The light turned green. Cammie yawned. "I think I'm worn down."

"A little shopping should revive you." Jules pointed at the red-and-white Lacy Lady sign. "We're here. And look, there's a parking space right in front."

As Cammie parallel parked, she made up her mind to enjoy herself. "Let's boogie," she said with enthusiasm.

Fifteen minutes later she plucked a hanger from a crowded rounder. "Do you think Kelly would like this?"

"Who cares about Kelly? We want something *Rick* will like," Jules said, laughing. She eyed the emerald-color, see-through teddy hanging from the hanger in Cammie's hand. "If you don't buy that, I will." An instant later her eyes widened. "You know, Cammie, that's a super color on you. Too bad…" The words trailed off.

"Too bad what?" Cammie prodded.

"Nothing. I just wish you had a man to wear that for."

No doubt Curt would love her in this teddy…. No! She wasn't going there, ever again. "This shopping trip isn't about me," she said firmly. "This teddy is for Kelly. Um, I mean, Rick."

"Holy Hanna, look at this." Jules plucked a purple garter and thong from the adjacent rack. "Do you think Steven will like me in this?"

"If he doesn't, he's crazy."

"Sold. What time does the bachelorette party start, and more important, when does the male stripper show up?" Jules asked as they headed for the cash register.

"It starts at seven." Kelly's best friend, Shashanna Porter, had offered her apartment for the festivities. "We'll drink cosmos while Kelly opens her gifts, then eat. The male stripper should arrive around nine." Unlike Todd, none of the women at this party would ever *dream* of sleeping with the entertainment.

That same night across town, Rick's friends were throwing him a similar party.

"Ooh-la-la." Jules fanned herself. "How I love bachelorette parties."

"You want to go in my place?"

Abruptly the laughter faded from Jules's eyes. "Are you sure you're over what happened?"

Though Todd's bachelor party had ended their wedding plans, and the humiliation had been horrible, Cammie nodded. "I truly am. The thing is, I've been doing so much lately that I'm simply not in a celebratory mood."

"No more than your usual workload." Jules eyed her with concern. "What's going on, Cammie?"

To tell or not to tell? Cammie bit her lip. "Well..."

The salesgirl looked curiously at Cammie. Not wanting anyone but Jules to know her personal business, Cammie waited until they exited the store.

The second the door shut behind them, Jules turned to her. "Talk."

"I went against my better judgment," Cammie said, clutching her purchase and lowering her voice. There weren't many people around, but you never knew. "I made love with Curt."

"What?!" Jules took her arm and pulled her into the doorway of another shop that had closed for the day. "I knew you were holding out on me! When? Where? I want details, and now."

"Calm down, Jules." Cammie gave her head a dismal shake. "It's not good."

The delight faded from Jules's expression. Her eyes narrowed. "Exactly what did he do? I may be in love with his brother, but I can still strangle him for you."

"This wasn't his fault." Cammie beckoned Jules closer. "I thought if I slept with Curt, I'd get him out of my system and at the same time get rid of this antsy, need-to-have-sex feeling that makes me seem overanxious." She gave Jules a sad smile. "Turns out, I was wrong."

"Oh, Cammie." Jules offered a sympathetic look. "Even I could have told you that."

"He knows me too well, Jules. Even though I never

so much as breathed the *L* word, he guessed. We fought about it. And that's that."

"How do you feel now?"

"Awful," Cammie admitted. "I'm still in love with him. But I'm bound and determined to get over this and move on."

"Forget dinner, and forget going home. I'm taking you out for a hot-fudge sundae at the Ice Cream Factory."

The last thing Cammie needed was ice cream. She thought of the pencil skirt she'd be wearing in nine days. Then she thought about her broken heart. She nodded. "You're on."

CERTAIN THAT THE DOUBLE-SCOOP hot-fudge sundae she'd eaten the night before had gone straight to her hips, Cammie decided she'd better show up at Thursday-night volleyball practice. So what if Curt would be there? As a mature adult she could face him.

"I am strong, I am invincible," she sang as she changed into a plum-color T-shirt and shorts. To underline her strength, she wore her scarlet underwear. *Eat your heart out, Curt.*

Yet for all her pep talk, the thought of seeing him was unnerving, and she sat on the bed, tugging on her gym socks with little enthusiasm. Far better to confront Curt now than at Kelly and Rick's rehearsal dinner a week from tonight, where Weston expected them to be warm and friendly to each other.

Warm and friendly, my foot. Under the circumstances, civility was the best Cammie could offer. That and convincing Curt that he was wrong, that she didn't love him.

Not one bit. That what they'd shared was nothing more than great, one-time-only sex.

She toed into her sneakers, bent over and tied the laces. Her goal for tonight was to show Curt she didn't care, and that no broken heart was going to keep her down. Ready to meet the challenge, she raised her head and marched to the living room to grab her purse.

Since she planned to come straight home after practice, no need to bring street clothes. Swinging the purse over her shoulder, she headed for the front door.

The sudden jangle of the phone cut through the silence. Cammie considered letting the machine pick up, but this might be important. Truth be told, she hoped it was important enough to keep her home from volleyball. At that cowardly thought, she snatched up the phone. "Hello?"

"Where the devil is Kelly?"

Cammie grimaced at Weston's demanding tone. "I don't know. We haven't talked since we came back from Portland two days ago." She frowned. "Why?"

"I've been calling her all day. No answer. Doesn't answer her door, either. Her car is parked in its usual slot, so where is she?"

Now he had Cammie wondering, too. "Did you check with Rick?"

"Of course I did," he said, as if she'd just asked the world's dumbest question. "Nobody's there, either."

"They probably went off somewhere together." For some much needed time away from Weston.

"Without telling me? That's not like my Kelly."

Cammie recalled Kelly's comment about eloping. She hoped they hadn't done that. "Weddings are stressful events, and stress can cause people to behave in strange ways. Maybe she needed a short break," Cammie said, hoping Weston got the point.

"That's total crap." Point not taken. "My daughter grew up in a house riddled with stress. She can handle anything, and you ought to know that."

Ignoring his contemptuous tone, Cammie glanced at her watch. If she didn't leave soon she'd be late for volleyball. She released an impatient sigh. "What is it you want?"

"Find her. Then let me know she's okay, so I can sleep tonight."

The man actually sounded worried, an emotion Cammie suspected was as foreign to him as fear of failure. She felt for him. "I'm sure she's okay," she soothed. "But I'll try my best."

"See that you do."

The phone clicked in her ear. So much for empathy. She dialed Kelly's cell. Kelly picked up on the first ring.

"Your father just called," Cammie said. "He's having a conniption. According to him, you're not home and you're not answering your phone."

"I'm screening my calls." Kelly's usual exuberant tone was subdued.

No doubt Weston had gone too far with some detail or demand. "What'd he do this time?" she asked.

"Who?"

"Your father, of course."

"Besides drive me crazy? Nothing. Hold on."

Cammie heard the unmistakable sound of Kelly blowing her nose. She frowned. "Kel? What's wrong?"

"Rick and I had a fight," Kelly said, her voice breaking.

She sounded utterly dejected. "What about?" Cammie asked, hurting for her friend.

"Eloping. Remember how you and I talked about that in Portland? I b-brought it up again Tuesday night, after we got back, and said I really wanted to. Rick took it all wrong. He said he knows me and if I don't want this wedding, maybe I don't want to get m-married at all." She let out a sob of despair. "He doesn't believe I want to marry him, Cammie. Now he's g-gone."

She was crying so hard, the words were difficult to understand. Not to mention Rick's skewed logic. Elopement meant you didn't want to get married?

"The w-wedding's off," Kelly blubbered.

The wedding's off. Cammie shuddered at those frightening words. Having suffered through her own canceled wedding, she wouldn't wish that trauma on an enemy, let alone sweet Kelly. Rick loved Kelly as deeply as she loved him, and they deserved to get married and spend the rest of their lives together.

"Brides and grooms go through this all the time," she said, hoping her words penetrated through Kelly's despair. "With all the stress of planning your wedding, it's almost inevitable that you'd fight about something. Especially in your case, with your father so involved in every little detail. Trust me, by tomorrow you and Rick will be fine, and this disagreement will be forgotten." She bit her lip. "Maybe you should call him?"

"I've tried, b-but he doesn't answer." Kelly sniffled. "I haven't seen or heard from him since he slammed the door late Tuesday night. We've never stayed mad at each other for this long." Fresh sobs broke out.

That didn't sound like Rick, and this was more serious than Cammie had guessed. Surprised and alarmed, she tried to think. "Did you stop by his house?"

"Several times. His car's gone, he doesn't answer his door, and Wednesday's and today's newspapers are still on the welcome mat." Kelly blew her nose again. "I drove by the track where he jogs, and the lab where he works. His last day is Friday, and they said he called in sick. He never calls in sick. I also checked the library, the Bar and Grill, Rosy's, even the hospital. I don't want people to know we're fighting, you know? You're the only one I've told." Her voice wavered. "Nobody's seen him." She went silent, and then a fresh sob filled the line. "That's why I can't take Daddy's calls. What'll I tell him?"

"Your father is worried sick," Cammie said. "He needs to know you're okay, but for the moment let's forget about him. "It's you I'm concerned about. I'm coming over." Recalling the comforting powers of her hot-fudge sundae the night before, she added, "With a carton of rum-raisin ice cream." Which was Kelly's favorite.

"I couldn't eat a thing right now," Kelly said.

"I'll bring some anyway."

Mind spinning, Cammie headed for her van, barely noting the misting rain. She hopped into her seat. If she could find Rick and get the two of them together, she had no doubt they'd work things out. But how to find him?

She needed help. Only one person came to mind. Curt. Forget her pride, this was more important. Without hesitation she pulled her cell phone from her purse and punched in his number, which she knew by heart.

He answered on the second ring. "Cammie?" he said in his deep voice.

"I need your help." In the beat of silence that fell she could sense his surprise. Heart thudding, she rushed on, quickly explaining the situation. "Can you find Rick and bring him to Kelly's?" she finished.

"Any idea where he might be?"

"If I knew that, I'd go get him myself." Worry made her sound testy to her own ears. "That wasn't nice," she apologized. "Kelly's already checked the hospital, the lab where he works and his favorite hangouts several times."

"Huh," Curt said.

She pictured him rubbing the back of his neck, the way he did when he was puzzled.

"She doesn't want people to know what's going on, so don't say anything."

"I won't," Curt said. "I'll be in touch."

TWO HOURS AFTER RECEIVING Cammie's call, Curt nudged Rick, who was unshaven and unwashed, up the dimly lit concrete steps of the small apartment complex where Kelly lived.

"Can't I at least clean up first?" Rick said, dragging his feet.

Curt had called Cammie, and she and Kelly were waiting. He shook his head. "They're expecting you now."

"But I need more time," Rick pleaded. He looked like a cornered animal, ready to bolt into the darkness.

Blocking the way down the stairs, Curt gestured with his chin at Kelly's door. "You can't run away, man. You and Kelly need to work things out."

Rick trudged toward the door, Curt behind him, his thoughts on Cammie. He realized he was talking to himself as well as Rick.

Which was ridiculous. There was nothing to work out with Cammie. They'd tried to be friends and had ended up in bed. End of story.

"Go on, ring the bell," he pushed.

Grumbling, Rick complied.

Within seconds, Cammie opened it. Her hair was curly and wild and she was wearing shorts and a T-shirt, light clothing for the chilly night.

"Hi, Rick," she said, widening the door. "Go on in."

Curt followed, and Cammie closed the door. They stayed back, out of the way.

"Is Rick okay?" she asked in a low voice.

"Time will tell," he replied, his gaze on the younger couple.

Pale and drained, Kelly sat hunched on the couch, hugging herself and working her lower lip between her teeth. She looked at Rick with a bleak expression that made Curt's chest hurt.

One look at her big, pain-filled eyes, and Rick was a goner. Making a low, anguished noise, he rushed to Kelly, who stumbled up to meet him.

Despite his filthy appearance, she opened her arms. They clung to each other, both crying and talking at once.

"I'm sorry—"

"I never should have left—"

"I think we're done here," Curt told Cammie.

"Kelly wanted me to stay, but I can see I'm not needed," she murmured. "I'm going home, Kelly," she said in a louder voice.

Kelly didn't appear to hear. She and Rick were locked in a fierce kiss not meant for anyone's eyes.

Smiling, Cammie grabbed her bag and slipped through the door. In silence, Curt walked beside her down the lit steps. In the brisk ocean air, gooseflesh dappled her arms. Her nipples poked against that shirt.

She might be cold, but he was warm. Too warm. Frowning, he shrugged out of his denim jacket and draped it around her shoulders. "It'll be cold for another month. Why are you dressed for summer?"

Slipping into the jacket, she shot him an exasperated look. "I was on my way to volleyball—"

"Volleyball." Curt smacked his forehead. "I forgot all about that." His gym bag was still at home, where he'd left it. He swore. "We both missed tonight. Now everyone will be talking about us."

The jacket was too big for her, and she looked small and cute. "Well, they'll be wrong," Cammie said, pushing up the sleeves.

She'd hinted at a subject he didn't want to visit—what had happened between them the other night. Dreading a discussion about love and heartbreak, Curt held his breath.

"I've missed so many practices and games now, they'll probably kick me off the team," she said.

Relieved that she hadn't gone where he was in no mood to go, he released his breath. "Hey, you had solid excuses. Next Thursday, we both will." The night of Rick and Kelly's rehearsal and the dinner that followed.

"All the same, I never really was interested in volleyball." They reached the parking lot and turned toward the visitor parking area. "I shouldn't have signed up. It was Jules's idea, a way to meet men." She gave a wry smile. "She did, too."

"You signed up to meet men? You said it was for the exercise."

A strange tension gripped Curt, square in the gut. He didn't understand why. Cammie *should* be out there, looking for a guy. But nobody in the volleyball league measured up. That was the only reason for the knot in his gut, he assured himself.

"Exercise, too," she said. "But it turns out I'm too busy for either. I am going to quit."

"Too bad. You're a great spiker."

"Flattery won't get you anywhere," she teased. "I suppose I should call Mike and make it official, huh?"

"I would." Curt spotted Cammie's car a dozen feet away.

"While Kelly and I waited for you and Rick, I made her call Weston," she said. "Poor man was worried sick."

"You don't see that often." Curt glanced at Cammie. "What'd she tell him?"

"That she had the flu. He wanted to come over but she said she wasn't up for company and promised to call him in the morning." Cammie slanted him a curious look. "Where on earth did you find Rick?"

"Believe it or not, at a campsite just outside town. He was holed up in a tent, reading *War and Peace* by flashlight. Apparently this is his third time reading the book."

"He was *reading? That?* You're kidding."

Curt shrugged. "Everybody escapes in their own way. At least it wasn't drugs or booze."

"He already smells bad enough," Cammie noted in a wry tone. "How did you know where he was?"

"Just a hunch. When Rick got his Eagle Scout badge, his parents hired me to photograph the ceremony. I must've been about twenty-three then, and heavy into hiking and camping. I remembered him saying he liked that particular site."

"I *knew* I could count on you," Cammie said, eyes shining under the parking lights. "Thanks."

Words Curt would have killed for mere weeks ago. Her appreciative smile dazzled him, and for a moment he wanted to pull her close and forget everything. But he'd already made that mistake, at a huge cost.

"No problem." He kept his expression bland. "How're you doing?"

Her eyes widened, and he swore he saw pain there. Then she blinked and looked away. "Very well, thank you."

Amazingly, she sounded as if she meant that. He must've imagined the hurt. Hardly aware of his actions, he peered closely at her face.

She actually smiled. "You don't have to worry about me, Curt. What happened the other night" She made a dismissive gesture. "I'm already over it."

She didn't love him after all? Curt wasn't sure he believed that. But she'd always worn her feelings on her face, and her casual expression seemed genuine.

How could she get over him so fast? He didn't like the way that felt, like a fist to the chest. "That's a relief," he muttered.

"Do you think they'll be okay?" she asked as they reached her car.

For a moment he couldn't recall who she meant. Then he remembered—Rick and Kelly. He nodded. "Rick invited me to his bachelor party on Saturday night, so I'd say the wedding's a go."

"That's good news. Well then, I'll see you a week from tonight at the rehearsal dinner. Thanks for the jacket." Cammie shrugged out of it and handed it to him, then pulled her key from the pocket in her purse and unlocked the car door. "Have a good week." She slid into her seat and closed the door.

Dismissed like the causal acquaintance he now was. Stung, shaking his head, Curt swore as he ambled toward his car.

As Cammie drove toward the exit, she honked and waved. Confused, his insides feeling weirdly tense again, he watched her drive off.

Clearly, she'd had a change of heart about him. Digging into the rear pocket of his jeans for his key, he frowned. He didn't understand her at all.

He understood himself even less.

Chapter Fourteen

Groggy and slightly hung over from Rick's bachelor party the night before, Curt parked in front of his father's place. He spotted Eric's and Steven's cars half a block away. Wouldn't you know they'd be on time. No doubt they'd razz him for showing up late.

They were here to do yard work and have dinner together, cooked by Kit and Eric. Most important, they meant to reassure the old man that the money for his operation was in the bank. Or would be, once Kelly and Rick got married and Weston paid Curt. Six days and counting.

The four pain-relief tablets Curt had taken had finally kicked in, and his head had just stopped pounding as he exited the car. It was a breezy, Sunday afternoon, and the tang of fresh ocean air that whipped his face felt good.

Besides the grass, the bushes could stand a good pruning, too. Despite his hangover, the thought of working up a sweat appealed to him.

Wiping his feet, he knocked. "It's me," he said before plowing through the door.

"About time you showed up," Steven replied from the living room.

He and Eric and Kit were crowded onto the sofa. The television was on with no sound. Curt nodded at his father, who looked like hell. He hid his worry under a smile. "Hey, Pop."

"Hi yourself. Grab a chair from the kitchen and sit down."

Curt hauled in a chair and placed it between his father and the rest of his family. "What'd I miss?"

"Nothing yet," Eric said. "We've been waiting for you."

Steven glanced at Curt and Eric, then acted the spokesman. "We want to talk about that operation, Pop. You're having it."

"The hell I am. I've already taken enough of you boys' money." Their father clamped his lips together.

"It's no big deal," Curt said. "I just got a check for that eighth-grade party, and after I finish the Atwood wedding I'll have plenty of cash. Pooled with what Steven, Eric and Kit have saved, there's enough for surgery and more physical therapy. No sweat."

When their father still looked skeptical, Steven set his jaw. "Remember what Dr. Scheyer said. If you don't have this surgery, you'll likely be in pain forever, and you'll end up in a wheelchair."

"Kit and I are with Steven," Eric said. "We vote yes on the operation."

"Vote? My medical issues are something to vote on?" Looking every bit as stubborn as Steven and Eric, their father crossed his arms and narrowed his eyes. "I see."

At this rate they'd never get Pop to come around. Curt eyed his father. "You know, if you're in a chair, it'd seriously cut down on chasing after women."

As he'd hoped, the old man cracked a smile. "Wouldn't want to disappoint the ladies."

Some of the tension faded from the room.

Kit, who had a way with their father, leaned forward, a hopeful look on her face. "Then you'll have the surgery?"

Holding their collective breath, they waited.

Their father sighed. "I don't like it, but I don't have much choice. Okay."

Everybody relaxed. Kit jumped up and hugged their pop, who chuckled and winced.

"I'll contact the doctor first thing tomorrow and let him know," Curt offered. "We'll get the operation scheduled right away."

"As long as it's after Weston Atwood pays you," his father said.

Curt shrugged. "Sure thing."

The big issue settled, his father's eyes narrowed. He sniffed the air. "I smell stale booze on you, Curt, which means a party." Interest gleamed in his eyes.

Eric, Kit and Steven also trained their attention on Curt. Damned if that wasn't annoying.

"I imagine you took my advice and did some of that skirt chasing yourself last night," their father continued. "Who is she?"

If only. Curt was in no mood to chase any woman. Not right now. He shook his head. "No females last night, Pop." Except for one anemic-looking stripper. "I was at Rick Mathers's bachelor party."

Their father looked surprised. "You haven't been to one of those since that mess with Todd. I hope Rick didn't take any strippers to bed." He winked. "But if he did, I hope he didn't get caught."

The statement defined every one of his pop's relationships with women. Which was sad, really. Curt shook his head. "It was a pretty tame event. The stripper was gone by midnight." The party had broken up shortly afterward.

"The male stripper at Kelly's party stayed until *two* and drank a cosmopolitan with the women before he left," Kit said.

News to Curt. "Where'd you hear that?"

She nodded at Steven. "From your brother."

"Jules told me," Steven said. "She talked to Cammie, who was there. According to her the guy was, and I quote, 'hunky, and really great at his job.' The ladies had a super time."

Curt imagined Cammie, ogling and salivating over the stripper, without a thought for Curt. Since she was over him, and all. Which was a good thing, he told himself. And scowled.

"Look at Curt's face." Steven rubbed his chin speculatively. "What's the deal?"

When Curt didn't reply, Eric did. "He's got a thing for Cammie."

Curt glared at him. "Don't you listen? I told you that's not true."

"Cammie, eh." Interest flared in their father's eyes. "She's a honey, all right." He shook his head. "All those years you were friends, I always wondered why you didn't go after her."

"Eric's wrong, Pop," Curt said. "Nothing's changed."

Except that they weren't even friends now, and he was seriously irritated that Cammie had gotten over him so fast. And confused as to why that bothered him.

His father opened his mouth. In no mood to talk further, Curt stood. "Let's get started on the lawn."

HALF AN HOUR BEFORE KELLY and Rick's wedding rehearsal, Cammie and Fran Bishop, owner of the Oceanside Bed and Breakfast, chatted in the great room. The spacious room was clean and orderly, and the floor-to-ceiling ocean-view windows were spotless. "Thanks for clearing out your guests for this," she said.

"No problem. They're excited about a wedding, and pleased to be invited to the reception after." Fran studied her face. "How are you doing? A wedding here can't be easy for you."

"It does feel weird," Cammie said, "but not as painful or uncomfortable as I imagined."

As long as she didn't think about Curt. She hadn't spoken to him since the night he'd brought Rick to Kelly's a week ago. For all her talk of moving on, it wasn't happening, and the big, empty hole in her heart refused to close. The one saving grace was she'd done a great job convincing Curt that she was over him.

Now, if she could convince herself…

"I'm relieved to hear that, and I just know you'll find the right man in due time." Fran's sympathetic expression echoed the words.

"Thanks." Cammie gestured out the window, where the ocean waves sparkled under blue skies and sunshine. "Let's hope the weather holds two more days. The sun setting over the ocean instead of clouds and rain would be so romantic. What time will the B and B crowd be back this afternoon?"

"Not for a nice, long while," Fran said. "Cinnamon

was kind enough to arrange a factory tour for my guests, followed by a stop at Cranberries-to-Go downtown, so they can sample the factory's wonderful new products," Fran continued. "Her husband picked them up in a van a little while ago. I don't expect them back for hours."

"We should be long gone by then," Cammie said. The rehearsal dinner, scheduled at a private golf club outside town, started in an hour and a half, and Weston would be on his ear to make that.

"I'm leaving, too, before Weston shows up and tries to boss *me* around." Long braid swishing down her back, Fran headed for the back door off the kitchen. "Have fun, and lock up when you finish."

Cammie wished she could follow Fran out. The past few days Weston had called her no fewer than five times a day to change details or check up on her. He'd changed tonight's dinner menu twice, the last time a few hours ago. She could almost feel her blood pressure rising. If she didn't love Kelly so much, and if Weston didn't buy insurance from her parents, she'd walk away.

Right. She'd never walked away from a job, and now was no time to get uppity. Two days and counting. Surely she could survive that.

Though after she and Kelly told Weston about canceling the fireworks… Dread filled her. She hoped that once he understood how important this was to Kelly, he'd let the matter drop. Regardless, he had to be told. Today. Right after the rehearsal.

As for Curt… She'd smile and go on pretending she didn't have feelings for him. She could survive that, too. Between dealing with Weston and overseeing the wedding, she'd be way too busy for much else.

Suddenly Curt was crossing the deck, along with the members of the string quartet hired for the processional. Behind him came Morley Adams, the friendly faced, balding minister, and Kelly, Rick and Weston. The four bridesmaids and groomsmen followed.

Time to act happy. Cammie pasted a bright smile on her face and opened the sliding door off the dining room to welcome them in.

With showing the quartet where she wanted them to set up, answering Weston's sixty zillion questions and groundless concerns and showing people where to stand, she barely had time to offer Curt a casual "hi" and a wave. But under the surface she was a sad mess of broken heart and longing. Curt didn't love her, but she couldn't help wishing he did.

The bright spot in the afternoon was Kelly and Rick. They were as lovey-dovey as ever. Thank goodness. Ready to get started, Cammie bustled toward them.

"Cammie!" Weston bellowed in a tone so hostile, she cringed.

Jaws dropped. Though the musicians bent to their instruments and the minister dipped his head to skim through his notes, the air grew heavy with tension.

Her stomach in knots, she pivoted to face Weston. Curt caught her eye and gave his head an ominous shake. He looked ready to punch out the man—for her. Though she genuinely appreciated the support, she motioned for him to calm down. He barely nodded, his eyes dark and narrowed, but she knew he'd do as she asked.

If only she could hold Weston to the same civil behavior. His eyes spit fire. His face was flushed, his jaw worked angrily. He was about to skewer her and she didn't even know why.

Her stomach lurched. "What is it?" she asked, doing her best to hide her fear.

"I just learned that you canceled the fireworks," he said in a loud, sharp tone that had her trembling inside. "After I specifically told you I wanted them. Either you're dumber than I thought, or you disobeyed me."

Now no one pretended to work. Shocked, they stared openly at him.

Refusing to let the man's fury get the best of her, Cammie managed a calm nod. "I was going to tell you about that after the rehearsal." She glanced at Kelly, whose face had gone pale. "If you recall, Kelly and Rick never wanted them. Kelly and I talked it over, and—"

"Shut up!"

"Daddy, please!" Kelly cried, covering her mouth with her hand.

"Cammie's telling the truth," Rick said, his face white and anxious. "She did what Kelly and I wanted, so don't blame her."

Weston quelled his daughter and future son-in-law with a furious scowl. He turned back to Cammie, whose whole body was shaking now. "You had no right to go behind my back, you stupid, disrespectful—"

"Watch your mouth, Atwood." Curt moved between her and Weston, his jaw clamped and his hands fisted at his sides.

For a split second Weston was too startled to respond. His expression darkened. "What did you say?"

Curt replied in a deadly quiet tone. "Either you treat Cammie with respect, or I quit."

COMMON SENSE TOLD CURT to back off and save his job. If not for him, for his father. But Weston had gone too far.

Cammie shot him a surprised look. "Don't Curt," she murmured, shaking her head. "You need this job."

"And you deserve respect," he said without taking his gaze from his boss.

Beet-red, hands clenched, Weston went nose to nose with Curt. "You little piece of—"

"Don't say it, or I'll quit, too," Cammie threatened.

Curt couldn't believe his ears. He darted her a curious look and received a tremulous smile.

Cammie had stuck up for him.

She cared, after all.

Despite the dire situation, his heart expanded in his chest. What the hell was happening to him? Thoroughly confused, he shook his head to clear it.

Oblivious, Weston frowned ominously from one to the other. "Nobody talks to me like that. Get out."

Sick at his stomach, Curt threw up his hands. "Fine." He turned to Cammie. "You coming?"

She bit her lip. Looked at Kelly. "I wanted to give you the best wedding ever, but with your father treating Curt and me like garbage, I just can't. I'm sorry, and I wish I hadn't talked you out of eloping. Maybe you should."

Stunned, Weston gaped at his daughter. "You wanted to elope?"

Kelly nodded miserably.

"But why?"

"Because you treat everybody as if they're lower than nothing. They're something to me, Daddy." Rick settled his arm around her. Kelly's gaze went round the room, stopping last on Curt and Cammie. "Especially Curt and

Cammie." She hung her head. "Right now, I'm ashamed to be your daughter."

Reeling as if he'd been slapped hard, Weston paled. He studied the floor. When he looked up moments later, he wore a genuinely contrite expression. "I've been a real son of a gun." He turned a regretful gaze on Kelly. "I'm sorry, honey."

Kelly crossed her arms. "Don't tell me, tell them."

Weston turned toward Cammie and Curt. He cleared his throat. "I was out of line, Cammie. You're smart and skilled and I should've trusted you. Curt, we both know you're the best photographer around. You can both stay."

Not the best apology in the world, but for Weston, quite a feat. Curt glanced at Cammie. She nodded. They were both still employed. Thank God. He blew out a breath. "Okay."

Everyone in the room, the minister included, applauded.

"Let's get on with it," Weston said. Then promptly glanced at Cammie. "If you're ready."

She smiled. "I most certainly am."

Chapter Fifteen

Accompanied by the string quartet, ushers directed guests to their seats. Camera at the ready on its tripod, Curt scanned the great room in amazement. The furniture had been pushed out of the way and the room transformed into a wonderland of flowers, with chairs and a white satin aisle up the center. Even the weather had cooperated. Rain was predicted late tonight, but at the moment the sky was clear and the room sunlit. The sliding doors were closed, though, keeping out any cool breezes. Guests chatted softly among themselves, and a smiling Reverend Adams clasped his book and stood waiting before the view windows.

Cammie glided toward Curt, her eyes bright with excitement. She was wearing a suit the color of deep pink roses that clung to her in all the right places, and matching strappy heels. Her hair had been styled into a sleek, sophisticated do, not a hint of curl, and her skin seemed to glow. She looked both hot and classy. "You look beautiful," he said.

"Thanks." A flush of pleasure colored her cheeks. Her gaze flitted over his black suit and gold tie. "Is that a new suit?"

He nodded. "Nice job with this room. I hardly recognize it."

"This is what Kelly wanted."

"No problems with Weston?"

"Not since you stuck up for me the other day. I owe you for that."

"Ditto."

Her eyes crinkled at the corners. She sent him a brilliant smile, and for an instant it was just like old times.

Except it wasn't. Since they'd faced down Weston Thursday, something inside Curt had shifted. His feelings for Cammie were different, warmer and more tender. Standing with her now, his chest seemed oddly full. He didn't understand, but he knew he couldn't survive without her in his life forever. As a close, trusted friend.

Hopefully she wanted the same. If they really tried, they could put the past behind them for good. No secrets between them. He'd even brought the proofs he'd taken of her that day at the Oceanside. If she wanted to destroy them, he would.

"Cammie—" he began.

A stir at the back of the room caught her eye. "Can it wait? I think they're ready."

"Sure," Curt said. They'd talk after the wedding.

She signaled the string quartet and took her seat in the front row on the bride's side of the room. The musicians struck up a new tune. Abruptly all conversation died. As the bridesmaids and groomsmen moved slowly up the aisle toward Reverend Adams and took their designated positions, Curt snapped a dozen photos. Looking nervous and excited, Rick joined the group. The music changed to the bridal march. The guests stood and turned to the back of the room.

Glowing and elegant in a shimmering veil and gown of white, Kelly clasped Weston's arm. For once he looked like a doting father, happy but at the same time filled with sadness that his little girl was about to join her life with a different man. They moved slowly and gracefully up the aisle. Curt snapped several photos, capturing Weston's bittersweet expression. He didn't like photos of himself smiling, but Curt figured he'd like these.

He glanced at Cammie, beaming through her tears. His chest aching with emotion, he captured that sweet, perfect expression on film. Then turned again to the wedding party.

Kelly joined Rick. Weston wiped his eyes and sat down beside Cammie, who handed him a tissue. Out of their mutual love for Kelly, any hostility between them had vanished.

While the couple exchanged vows, Curt snapped photos. The awe and reverence on Rick's face was something to see. Curt understood—he felt similar strong emotions for Cammie. Zooming in, he captured the look for posterity. Fueling the awe and reverence was pure, abiding love.

Curt knew that feeling, too. Like a bolt of lightning, realization hit him. He loved Cammie.

His heart felt as if it would burst from his chest, and for a moment he couldn't move or think. Then he remembered. He was a Blanco, and Blanco men were not built for love. Not the kind that lasted.

Damn, damn and damn. He'd always prided himself

on common sense, but in the end he was no better than Steven, Eric or their father. Then again…

Eric claimed his love for Kit was "for real," and so far, so good. And Steven seemed to be following suit with Jules, though time would tell. As for the old man, he was a lost cause and always would jump from woman to woman.

But Curt himself… Now that he'd owned up to the truth, he realized he'd loved Cammie since that first kiss in the coat closet, for more than seventeen years. If that didn't mean he was a one-woman man, nothing did. He wasn't like his pop, after all.

He was so stunned, he almost missed Kelly and Rick's kiss. Luckily it lasted a while and he managed to get some great shots.

All of a sudden he couldn't wait for the wedding and reception to end. He couldn't wait to tell Cammie he loved her. But she didn't feel the same way about him. Her love for him had come and gone. Depressing as hell, but Curt wouldn't let that stop him.

If it was the last thing he did, he'd convince her that he was the right man for her.

WEDDING OVER AND GUESTS GONE at last, Cammie stood on the deck that faced the ocean. The sky had clouded up, but the weather had held for the wedding. Now the tide was coming in and the rhythm of the waves as they licked the beach was soothing and relaxing. Flying low over the water, gulls and pelicans circled restlessly in search of dinner. Cold—the early evening air was brisk—but she was unwilling to leave just yet, and inhaled a breath of sea air, released it and felt the tension ebb from her body.

What a perfect wedding it had been, filled with joy and happiness during the ceremony and the reception.

Now Kelly and Rick, radiant as man and wife, were on their way to the airport for a ten-day honeymoon in Fiji. Weston, who had thanked Cammie and paid her, had taken relatives and close friends to his house for their own private celebration.

The kitchen was clean, the great-room furniture back in place, and all signs of the wedding gone. Fran's bed-and-breakfast guests had left, no doubt to enjoy Cranberry at night. Fran herself had disappeared to her apartment downstairs.

Cammie was alone. No one to go home to, talk over today or share the evening with.

Would it always be this way?

A raindrop pelted her cheek. As she turned and hurried for the sliding door, it opened. Curt stood there. She knew she looked surprised.

"Better get in here," he said. "You don't want that fancy hairdo to frizz." He moved aside to let her in.

"I thought you'd left."

"I packed up my stuff, ditched the tie and jacket and came back." He slid the door closed behind her, shutting out the cold air. "With these." He nodded at a large brown envelope on the dining-room table. "We need to talk."

Ominous words, and they distracted her from the envelope. Dread filled her. "Haven't we done enough of that already?" she said, steeling herself for whatever he might say.

"Indulge me."

At the beseeching look on his face and the soft light in

his eyes, her wariness faded. Her traitorous heart opened, and she wondered whether she'd ever stop loving him. She nodded. "What did you want to say?"

"You did an amazing job today. I got some beautiful shots that ought to make Weston and the family happy."

"That's great," Cammie said. Was this what he wanted to talk about? "If that's all, we should leave now."

"You haven't looked in the envelope." He nodded toward the table.

"Those are proofs, right?"

"From the parties and Kelly's shower."

At the moment, the last thing she wanted to do was look at pictures of Kelly and Rick. "Shouldn't you give these to the family?"

"I doubt they'd be interested. These are from my private stash."

She couldn't muster a hint of enthusiasm. "Can't it wait?"

"You look stressed." Curt frowned. "Hey, the wedding's over, and Weston paid us both. Why aren't you smiling?"

"Because it's over." *And I want what Kelly has.* "No more adrenaline rush. Did you know they're going to Fiji for their honeymoon?"

"Rick told me," Curt said. He angled his chin. "Where do you want to go on yours?"

"You mean if I ever get married?" Her laugh sounded as hollow as it felt. "I always wanted to go to Italy. Tuscany and the Amalfi Coast."

Pensive, he nodded. He'd always been a good listener. She loved him so much, but in time she'd get over him. She would. Even if Curt could never love her, he was important to her and she needed him in her life. Now was the time to tell him so.

"Curt—"

"Cammie—"

They started at the same time. He grinned, and so did she, a real smile that felt good.

"Me first," he said. He slid the envelope toward her. "Open it."

She frowned.

"Just open it."

He stood across the table while she straightened the fastener on the back of the envelope. She slid out the pages of black-and-white proofs, every photo featuring her. Her foot, her leg, her ankle and the tattoo over it. Her face, smiling, sober, pleased, exasperated. The artsy pictures made her look natural and attractive. Sultry even.

"What do you think?" Looking like a man with his life on the line, Curt stabbed his hand through his hair.

Why?

"They're very good. And flattering." Puzzled, she eyed him. "Why did you take them?"

"At the time I hardly knew myself. Now…" He shifted and cleared his throat. Stuck his fingers in his unbuttoned collar as if it were too tight. "Watching Rick and Kelly today, I realized something huge." His gaze sought hers. "I love you, Cammie."

Certain she'd misheard, she stared dumbly at him. "What?"

"I love you."

Mind spinning, she widened her eyes. "I thought you didn't believe in love."

"I was wrong."

Still confused, she frowned. "But I want to get married and settle down, and you aren't cut out for long-term relationships."

"That's what I used to believe." He moved from the other side of the table to stand before her. "The truth is, I've loved you for seventeen years. If that isn't long-term..." He swallowed audibly. "I want to spend my life with you. And make pretty, blond babies. Lots of them."

She opened her mouth. Curt grabbed her hands and rushed on, as if he were afraid of what she might say.

"I know you only loved me a little, right after we made love. But if you give me the chance I'll treat you so well, you're bound to fall in love with me again. I hope," he finished under his breath.

Heart overflowing, Cammie squeezed his hands, which were trembling. "I never stopped loving you, you big lug."

The astonished look on his face was priceless.

"But you said...you acted like..."

"So I deserve an Academy Award for pretending I was over you. I love you, Curt Blanco, and I always will." She dropped his hands to twine her arms around his neck. "Now kiss me."

"Jeez, you're bossy," he quipped, his face warm with feeling.

He claimed her lips in a deliciously tender kiss. Her heart full, she melted against him.

Moments later he pulled back, keeping his arms around her. "I feel like I just won the lotto. Wahoo!"

He laughed, a big, warm sound that vibrated through her. Cammie, too, laughed. When they both sobered, Curt rested his forehead on hers.

"Does this mean we can work together again?" She nodded, and he grinned. "How does Blanco and Blanco, Events Planning and Photography sound to you?"

"If that's a proposal, the answer is I do."

"Thank God."

His eyes grew suspiciously bright. Cammie's eyes filled, too. Oh, how she loved this man.

"When do you want to do it?" she asked. "And where?"

"Any place you want, as soon as my father is well enough. That should give me the time to book us a trip to Italy and you the chance to plan the wedding."

"I want to get married here at the Oceanside," she said. Her mind busy, she pushed out of his arms. "We'll have to work around my schedule and Fran's. Better grab my BlackBerry and check dates. Wait'll my parents hear about this! Won't they be surprised when I pick them up next week? I'll contact the caterers and—"

"Later," Curt interrupted. "Right now, there are more important matters."

Cupping her shoulders, he pulled her close again and kissed her. This kiss was deeper and more passionate. Fire ignited in her body, and she knew that they could easily make love right here in Fran's dining room. With guests coming and going, not a wise idea.

As if he read her thoughts, he broke contact, chest heaving. "Let's get out of here. I'll drive."

Breathless, she nodded. "We can pick up my car later. My house is closer than yours. Let's go there."

He snatched the photos. In short time he handed

Cammie her purse, grabbed her hand and pulled her to-ward the sliding door. "I want to take you home and make love with you all night long."

And he did.

* * * * *

Watch for
FRAN'S STORY,
Ann Roth's next book
set in Cranberry, Oregon,
coming August 2007,
only from Harlequin American Romance!

*Set in darkness beyond the ordinary world.
Passionate tales of life and death.
With characters' lives ruled by laws the everyday
world can't begin to imagine.*

n⬤cturne

It's time to discover the Raintree trilogy...

New York Times bestselling author
LINDA HOWARD
brings you the dramatic first book
RAINTREE: INFERNO

*The Ansara Wizards are rising and the Raintree clan
must rejoin the battle against their foes, testing their
powers, relationships and forcing upon them lives
they never could have imagined before...*

*Turn the page for a sneak preview
of the captivating first book
in the Raintree trilogy,
RAINTREE: INFERNO by **LINDA HOWARD**
On sale April 2.*

Dante Raintree stood with his arms crossed as he watched the woman on the monitor. The image was in black-and-white to better show details; color distracted the brain. He focused on her hands, watching every move she made, but what struck him most was how uncommonly *still* she was. She didn't fidget or play with her chips, or look around at the other players. She peeked once at her down card, then didn't touch it again, signaling for another hit by tapping a fingernail on the table. Just because she didn't seem to be paying attention to the other players, though, didn't mean she was as unaware as she seemed.

"What's her name?" Dante asked.

"Lorna Clay," replied his chief of security, Al Rayburn.

"At first I thought she was counting, but she doesn't pay enough attention."

"She's paying attention, all right," Dante murmured. "You just don't see her doing it." A card counter had to remember every card played. Supposedly counting cards was impossible with the number of decks used by the casinos, but there were those rare individuals who could calculate the odds even with multiple decks.

"I thought that, too," said Al. "But look at this piece of tape coming up. Someone she knows comes up to her and speaks, she looks around and starts chatting, completely misses the play of the people to her left—and doesn't look around even when the deal comes back to her, just taps that finger. And damn if she didn't win. Again."

Dante watched the tape, rewound it, watched it again. Then he watched it a third time. There had to be something he was missing, because he couldn't pick out a single giveaway.

"If she's cheating," Al said with something like respect, "she's the best I've ever seen."

"What does your gut say?"

Al scratched the side of his jaw, considering. Finally, he said, "If she isn't cheating, she's the luckiest person walking. She wins. Week in, week out, she wins. Never a huge amount, but I ran the numbers and she's into us for about five grand a week. Hell, boss, on her way out of the casino she'll stop by a slot machine, feed a dollar in and walk away with at least fifty. It's never the same machine, either. I've had her watched, I've had her followed, I've even looked for the same faces in the casino every time she's in here, and I can't find a common denominator."

"Is she here now?"

"She came in about half an hour ago. She's playing blackjack, as usual.

"Bring her to my office," Dante said, making a swift decision. "Don't make a scene."

"Got it," said Al, turning on his heel and leaving the security center.

Dante left, too, going up to his office. His face was

calm. Normally he would leave it to Al to deal with a
cheater, but he was curious. How was she doing it?
There were a lot of bad cheaters, a few good ones, and
every so often one would come along who was the stuff
of which legends were made: the cheater who didn't get
caught, even when people were alert and the camera was
on him—or, in this case, her.

It was possible to simply be lucky, as most people understood luck. Chance could turn a habitual loser into
a big-time winner. Casinos, in fact, thrived on that hope.
But luck itself wasn't habitual, and he knew that what
passed for luck was often something else: cheating. And
there was the other kind of luck, the kind he himself possessed, but it depended not on chance but on who and
what he was. He knew it was an innate power and not
Dame Fortune's erratic smile. Since power like his was
rare, the odds made it likely the woman he'd been watching was merely a very clever cheat.

Her skill could provide her with a very good living,
he thought, doing some swift calculations in his head.
Five grand a week equaled $260,000 a year, and that
was just from his casino. She probably hit them all,
careful to keep the numbers relatively low so she stayed
under the radar.

He wondered how long she'd been taking him, how
long she'd been winning a little here, a little there, before Al noticed.

The curtains were open on the wall-to-wall window
in his office, giving the impression, when one first
opened the door, of stepping out onto a covered bal-
cony. The glazed window faced west, so he could catch
the sunsets. The sun was low now, the sky painted in

purple and gold. At his home in the mountains, most of
the windows faced east, affording him views of the sunrise. Something in him needed both the greeting and the
goodbye of the sun. He'd always been drawn to sun-
light, maybe because fire was his element to call, to
control.

He checked his internal time: four minutes until sun-
down. Without checking the sunrise tables every day, he
knew exactly when the sun would slide behind the
mountains. He didn't own an alarm clock. He didn't
need one. He was so acutely attuned to the sun's position
that he had only to check within himself to know the
time. As for waking at a particular time, he was one of
those people who could tell himself to wake at a certain
time, and he did. That talent had nothing to do with being Raintree, so he didn't have to hide it; a lot of perfectly ordinary people had the same ability.

He had other talents and abilities, however, that did
require careful shielding. The long days of summer in-
stilled in him an almost sexual high, when he could feel
contained power buzzing just beneath his skin. He had
to be doubly careful not to cause candles to leap into
flame just by his presence, or to start wildfires with a
glance in the dry-as-tinder brush. He loved Reno; he
didn't want to burn it down. He just felt so damn *alive*
with all the sunshine pouring down that he wanted to let
the energy pour through him instead of holding it inside.

This must be how his brother Gideon felt while pulling lightning, all that hot power searing through his
muscles, his veins. They had this in common, the con-
nection with raw power. All the members of the far-
flung Raintree clan had some power, some heightened

ability, but only members of the royal family could channel and control the earth's natural energies.

Dante wasn't just of the royal family, he was the Dranir, the leader of the entire clan. "Dranir" was synonymous with king, but the position he held wasn't ceremonial, it was one of sheer power. He was the oldest son of the previous Dranir, but he would have been passed over for the position if he hadn't also inherited the power to hold it.

Behind him came Al's distinctive knock on the door. The outer office was empty, Dante's secretary having gone home hours before. "Come in," he called, not turning from his view of the sunset.

The door opened, and Al said, "Mr. Raintree, this is Lorna Clay."

Dante turned and looked at the woman, all his senses on alert. The first thing he noticed was the vibrant color of her hair, a rich, dark red that encompassed a multitude of shades from copper to burgundy. The warm amber light danced along the iridescent strands, and he felt a hard tug of sheer lust in his gut. Looking at her hair was almost like looking at fire, and he had the same reaction.

The second thing he noticed was that she was spitting mad.

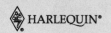

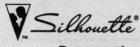

Romantic
SUSPENSE

**Sparked by Danger,
Fueled by Passion.**

*This month and every month look for
four new heart-racing romances
set against a backdrop of suspense!*

Available in May 2007

Safety in Numbers
(Wild West Bodyguards miniseries)
by **Carla Cassidy**

Jackson's Woman
by **Maggie Price**

Shadow Warrior
(Night Guardians miniseries)
by **Linda Conrad**

One Cool Lawman
by **Diane Pershing**

Available wherever you buy books!

Visit Silhouette Books at www.eHarlequin.com   SRS0407

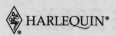

HARLEQUIN®

American | ROMANCE®

A THREE-BOOK SERIES BY BELOVED AUTHOR

Judy Christenberry

Dallas Duets

What's behind the doors of
the Yellow Rose Lane apartments?
Love, Texas-style!

THE MARRYING KIND

May 2007

Jonathan Davis was many things—a millionaire,
a player, a catch. But he'd never be a husband.
For him, "marriage" equaled "mistake." Diane Black
was a forever kind of woman, a babies-and-minivan
kind of woman. But John was confident he could
date her and still avoid that trap.
Until he kissed her…

Also watch for:

DADDY NEXT DOOR

January 2007

MOMMY FOR A MINUTE

August 2007

Available wherever Harlequin books are sold.

REQUEST YOUR FREE BOOKS!
2 FREE NOVELS PLUS 2
FREE GIFTS!

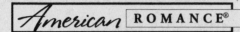

Heart, Home & Happiness!

HAR07

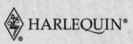

HARLEQUIN®

American ROMANCE®

COMING NEXT MONTH

#1161 THE MARRYING KIND by Judy Christenberry
Dallas Duets
Jonathan Davis was many things—a millionaire, a player, a catch. But he'd
never be a husband. For him, "marriage" equaled "mistake." Diane Black was a
forever kind of woman, a babies-and-minivan kind of woman. But John was
confident he could date her and still avoid that trap. Until he kissed her…

#1162 THE TEXAS RANGER by Jan Hudson
Texas Outlaws
Sam Bass Outlaw knew from the first moment he laid eyes on Skye Walker that
he had to get to know her—although the beautiful blonde was hard to get close
to, considering the German shepherd, bodyguards and overprotective brother.
Whatever Skye's story was, this Texas Ranger would find out!
Meet the Outlaws—a Texas family dedicated to law enforcement

#1163 DADDY PROTECTOR by Jacqueline Diamond
Fatherhood
Connie Simmons's neighbor Hale Crandall is wildly attractive, totally
irresponsible and doesn't have a serious thought in his head. But after
witnessing his heroic rescue of the child she's about to adopt, she realizes
she might be wrong. Especially once the unpredictable detective starts to
prove he's deadly serious about her!

#1164 ALEGRA'S HOMECOMING by Mary Anne Wilson
Shelter Island Stories
For Alegra Reynolds, returning home means showing everyone how successful
she's become. For Joe Lawrence, Shelter Island on Puget Sound is a safe haven
for him and his son. Will these opposites learn that home has less to do with the
tiny island they were born on and more to do with each other?

www.eHarlequin.com

HARCNM0407